CW01498613

Of Humans &
Other Creatures
and a lady with two brains

Book II

Every Picture Tells a Story

Amanda Brooks

FEB 2024

First published in 2023 by Amanda Brooks

Text and illustrations
©Amanda Brooks 2023

ISBN: 9781999703158 print
ISBN: 9781999703141 ebook

This edition printed and bound by Ingram Spark

You may or may not have read Book I, My Desperate Year, if not why not? This would be a good time to put that right, otherwise this second book may be more confusing that it need be . . .

Dedicated in loving memory to my Mum Jane Brooks, and to the faithful few who have stalwartly believed that I would get on with it and produce this book, which was written some time ago, but which got swept away in a tidal wave of otherness.

This is definitely not the end – Book III is in the making . . . kindly hold on.

Introduction

Upon entering The Little White House folk soon became aware that they were somewhere strangely quite different. Not different because a chill (suggesting ancient spirits) hit them, but because the inside was not exactly as the outside suggested.

The outside was rather ordinary - in a nice and pleasant way, but the inside . . .

Inside, on every wall and in each available space hung a picture or lived a sculpture - it was lovely, if you like that kind of thing.

* * *

But. As much as The Little White House continued to grow as a safe and peaceful haven, and as much as the lady was happy in her new space, she knew that changing one thing doesn't necessarily change anything else and she still had to earn her living. She continued her quest to find new shop premises. She viewed so many but was invariably pipped at the post by chains of coffee shops, or worse still estate agents. Grrrrhhhhh.

And soon, and sure enough, and to her dismay, the money in the pot was diminishing, and she began to wonder how she was going to cope. 'Get some help,' said the brother. So the lady embarked on a new journey, although she couldn't help feeling she had been there and here before. She would need all her strength to get through this next, new bit, and would have to call upon her other brain to help her.

That being said, The Little White House continued to bring joy, and as the lady wandered from room to room she gazed deeply into the pictures that she and Little Lily had hung together, and each one told a very different story . . .

I sit and ponder in my now house. The house which I sometimes consider to be my now 'downgraded' space. And I think about the trouble in the world . . . and I think about a neighbour who left for work one morning and dropped dead from a heart attack. And I wonder how dare I sometimes feel hard done by.

There's food and wine in the fridge and, thank you Lord, those I love are well and happy. So why is change and acceptance so hard?

Before I left 'the big house' one of my friends said 'Amanda, you can only sleep in one bed at a time.'

How true.

So I am more than grateful for what I now have and that's about it . . . But that led me to wonder whether I am chasing rainbows? Possibly, but isn't it good to strive and not give in too readily to complacency? And isn't it something to wonder about the wonder?

I didn't know that this particular wondering would bring us here . . . but it did.

Goodbye to a Rainbow . . .

The Top Landing

Goodbye to a Rainbow
A Tricky Conversation between the Colours

A quivering colour oozed from the gloom, crossed, and hovered, somewhat menacingly, in front of another.

'I want out,' said Red.

'Out? What do you mean, out?'

'Out. Away from the group.'

'Out? Away from the group?'

'Yes. Out. Away from the group.'

'But you can't get out and away from the group, as you put it.'

'I can and I will.'

'No, Red, no. You can't. For we are one.'

'Blast you Indigo. I am over you. I am over you all. I want out.'

'But you cannot be 'over us' as you say. We only exist when we are together.'

'Damn stupid idea that was.'

'Not really Red . . . it has always been thus.'

'And now I want a change.'

'Why? And why now?'

'I am bored.'

'Bored?'

'Yes, bored. Bored bored bored. Bored. Gettit?'

'Well no, not really. How can you be bored? Don't you love the wonderful way we look as a group?'

'Nah.'

'The way the light filters through us and makes us shimmer?'

'Nah.'

'The thrill we give to humans when they witness our arc?'

'Nah.'

'The way . . . what do you want Red?'

'I want to be alone.'

'Alone?'

'Yes.'

'Alone?'

'Yes.'

'Why?'

'Haven't you ever wanted to break out?'

'No.'

'No. I suppose you haven't. Why, you . . . you Indigo. You are petty and submissive.'

'No, I just know my place.'

'Yes yes, and yours is always the same place - between Blue and Violet.'

'Nothing wrong with that.'

'Look. I have the longest wavelength and I should be allowed to do as I please.'

'Well it doesn't really work like that.'

'I don't care. I wish to leave.'

'Red, firstly I don't think it is physically possible for you to leave, secondly, were it possible, it would cause much consternation to the humans and other creatures and thirdly, where would you go?'

'The fields.'

'The fields?'

'Yep.'

'Why?'

'Red sky.'

'Eh?'

'Red sky.'

'What do you mean 'Red sky'?'

'I intend to be a Red sky. On my own. Alone.'

'Because?'

'Because I wish to delight and warn the shepherds.'

'Red, Red, Red . . .'

'And what's wrong with that as an alternative life plan?'

'It is a fine life plan Red, but we are not that sort of substance. You can't just get out. We live together and we only exist when conditions are right.'

'Who decided that?'

'Some would say The Creator and some would say The Big Bang.'

'Whaddayou think?'

'I do not know Red.'

'You do not know?'

'No, I do not know, yet I choose to believe in The Creator.'

'Right. Let's go and see The Creator then.'

'We can't.'

'What do mean we can't?'

'We do not know whether or not The Creator exists.'

'And yet it is because of this Creator that we are bound together?'

'Some would say, yes.'

'Yet we cannot see him, visit for a cuppa?'

'No Red. No.'

'Well what a liberty.'

Indigo sighed.

'Right. That's it. I'm off,' said Red. 'Now, if I could just disengage my foot . . .'

'But you don't have a foot Red. You are merely a haze in the fracturoscope of vision.'

'Eh?' said Red, struggling to disentangle the 'end' of him.

'The edge of a vapour cloud. The difference between air and nothingness. The way that air and water and heat and moisture behave, when all together . . .'

'Whatever, I am going to break free.'

'You won't do it, Red. It isn't possible.'

'Damn you Indigo.'

* * *

'Hmm,' said Indigo. 'Looks like rain. Gather round, wake up Violet. Places everyone and . . .'

Overhead the rain clouds had indeed gathered, yet in the distance the sun could be seen blaring out its yellow warmth and light. Always the light. The colours stood up and shook themselves. Time for the performance.

Sure enough, the sun shone down on them and through the rain the wonderful apparition was seen by the humans and other creatures below.

'Wow,' said the humans. And 'Look look Mum, a Rainbow.'

The performance lasted a good fifteen minutes until the clouds, bullish and swollen with rain and in a rush to spill their loads, managed to screen out the sun completely. The rainbow was no more.

'I do so love that. Don't you love that Red? Don't you love that moment, for however long it lasts, when we are the Kings of the Universe, seemingly, and everyone is looking at us?'

'No.'

'When humans stop in their tracks and get out of their cars and gaze upon us and say 'Wow'?'

'No.'

'You do not like that Red?'

'No.'

'And what about the Pot of Gold? Do you not like the story of the Pot of Gold?'

'No.'

'But where would that story be were there no rainbows?'

'There is no pot of gold Indigo.'

'You don't think so?'

'No. You know that there is not one, and I know that and so do the others. Pot of Gold indeed. What a load of nonsense.'

'But it's metaphorical Red.'

'Eh?'

'It's metaphorical. No one, not even the humans, truly believe there is an actual pot of gold at the end of a rainbow, but whilst humans and other creatures seek it, they may not find what they want, but they might just find what they need.'

'What are you banging on about?'

'Look, the humans and other creatures may decide to hunt for the metaphorical pot of gold on an afternoon, say, with their children, and whilst seeking they may discover that it is all good fun, and that the Dad likes the Mum after all, say, and that running around the slightly damp fields in an afternoon is better than watching another episode of Downton, and that being together and breathing the air has value as they have stopped listening to their techno rubbish for a while, and . . .'

'Yes yes . . . I get the picture.'

'So you see Red, you see that we are not merely a group of random colours brought together for the occasional moment of glory before disappearing into the clouds again.'

'We aren't?'

'No Red. We are the Bringers of Hope. We were forged together by The Creator or The Masters of The Universe to show the Wonder of Things to the humans and other creatures below. We inspire them to write poetry and music when they behold our beauty. We form part of the Orchestra of the Wonder of the Skies. For we are a wonder Red, never forget that . . . Why Red, without us the world would be a mighty sight more glum.'

'Blimey.'

'Yes Red, blimey.'

Red sat down on a whisp. He was slightly blown away by Indigo's outpouring.

'Red. Your alternative life plan of delighting and warning shepherds is a great one, but don't you see how much more valuable you are as part of the team?'

'Ummmmm . . .'

'Red - together we do not simply delight and warn a few random shepherds stuck out on some grassy hillock. NO! Together we are little short of a Miracle!'

Indigo stood perfectly still, vapour arms extended. He wiped a tear from his eye. He knew that Red could not actually leave (unless of course he made an application to The Creator or The Masters of The Universe, which requisition could take some time he imagined) but he wanted Red to stay because he wanted to stay. And he needed Red's solidarity if he himself were to continue to believe in the performances . . .

'So Red. Are you in or are you in?'

'I am IN.'

The two colours fused together for a fizzling moment. Indigo let out a huge sigh of relief. He

turned. He felt the need for a lie down - besides
which he had spotted another storm approaching.

'Indigo?'

'Yes Red?'

'Thanks.'

'Any time.'

'And Indigo?'

'Yes Red?'

'Together Forever?'

'Yes Red.'

Together Forever

The Elf knew that all was not right . . . she could feel it and see it in the way that all the stars in her wand were stuck at the bottom. She loved The Little White House and felt safe and happy, but still there was the overwhelming feeling that all was not right. What to do? What to do? She was tired, and at times it was hard not to simply sit down and put her head in her hands and stay like that for a very long time . . . but then what would happen? Besides, she was renowned for being a Bundle of Energy and this was no time to shie away from difficulties. She knew all about difficulties. 'Stand tall' her Hermit Elf Grandfather would have said 'and march like a soldier, and' he would have added 'remember little one, we do not take prisoners.'

The Bundle of Energy

'You're a bundle of energy' some of the Elf's friends would say to her. Or people would comment on it to each other when she was busy flying and flitting around doing all the sorts of things she did in a day.

But actually it wasn't that she was a bundle of energy, it was because she had a Bundle of Energy and most days she started with a full one.

When her Bundle of Energy was full it was like a great big sack of potatoes but without the knobblyness of potatoes. But when the Bundle was empty it was flat, like a cushion cover without the cushion inside. The Bundle wasn't heavy to carry around like the Weight of Uncertainty which she sometimes had to carry, now that was heavy, and most days she managed pretty well.

On the days when she had a full Bundle, she had no problem giving bits of the energy away to friends or to tidying and sorting or to general busyness. But on days when the Bundle was feeling rather squeezed out, she had very little to give.

'Why don't you save some of the Energy for yourself?' her Hermit Elf Mother had often asked her. 'You sometimes give too much away and then you are as flat as the pancakes made on Shrove Tuesday.'

The Elf would smile to herself, inwardly of course, as her Hermit Elf Mother was a fine one to talk - she gave her Energy away too, but over time had learned to keep a weeny bit for herself which she carried in the inside pocket of her tunic for 'Just in Case' moments.

But then her Hermit Elf Mother was very wise.

That particular morning, over a refreshing cup of mint and honeysuckle tea, the Elf thought about her Bundle of Energy and decided to try a new approach with it. She would make a List, which she loved to do, and try to ensure that she *gave just the right amount of Energy to the right amount of things.*

'Let's see,' she thought. 'Fruity Bat Fly and Ronie are visiting this morning so I'll need to use this much Energy.' She made a two dollop mark on her List.

'Then I must run around looking for Inspiration, and that will take this much Energy.' She made a one dollop mark on her List.

'Oh, then there are the books to take back to the Owls, and I promised to clean their staircase . . .' the List was getting more and more dollopy.

'And then I must try and work out if I can finally find a shop. Hmm. That'll probably need this much Energy.' She drew a very large double-dollop on her list. (The shop was something she had wanted to do for a long time. She intended to collect things from anyone who wanted to give their things away and then give their things to other people who needed those things. A sort of re-sorting place. But not like Robin Hood.)

She looked at the List and realised that all those things would take up most of the Energy she had found in the Bundle when she had got up that morning.

'Better get on then,' she thought. She tied up the Bundle, folded the List and put it in her pocket, and at that moment Fruity Bat Fly and Ronie arrived at the house. As always they were a complete joy and they all had great fun playing water games in the garden, jumping off the beds and painting funny other faces on their faces. When their Mother Little Scottie came to pick them up they were all very happy, almost hysterical, and terribly hungry. Little Scottie whisked

them off down the road, waving as they hopped and tripped back to where they were staying.

And the Elf had indeed used up the two dollops.

'Right. Now where is that Inspiration?' The Elf knew it was somewhere to be found, and she usually found it, but some days it just couldn't be found and all she actually found was that she would have been better off not looking so hard in the first place, and she would have probably found it anyway.

Another dollop gone.

The Elf slung the Bundle of Energy over her shoulder and gathered up the books she wanted to return to the Owls. She skipped off into the woods and soon arrived at the Owls' home. Knowing they would be asleep, as it was daytime, she crept up the no-longer-rickety staircase (which had been mended before a party they had recently thrown) and popped the books down at the end of the Owls' branch. She then picked up an Owl feather duster and started to clean the staircase, descending it as she cleaned. But the staircase was a long and winding one and it was hard work. 'Come on, keep going,' she said to herself, 'otherwise this hard day will turn into a hard days' night.' And she flicked the duster and rubbed away at the blobs of spent shrewskin and kept going until she reached the bottom step.

Her Bundle of Energy was deflating, as was she. She knew she had given away a bit too much of it helping the Owls, but then she loved them so.

When she got home she sat down and thought about her use of Energy. Energy was a funny old thing - why is it *that on some days you seem to have more than enough and on others it runs out too quickly?*

Sometimes it seemed that no matter how much Energy she used up or handed out there was still loads left inside. On those days she had to be very careful when she got home as too much Energy, left unused, has a habit of oozing out of the Bundle demanding more action, and then it is very hard to sleep.

Sometimes it seemed that it ran out very quickly indeed, without you feeling that you had done anything.   On those days she felt squeezed out like the bagpipes her friend Mack in Togs had played, squeezed out after a particularly long note.   And you never woke up in the morning knowing how long the Energy would last.   And you couldn't not do all the things you had planned.   On those days you had to borrow some of the next days' Energy - which meant you were often in debit.

She looked at her List and compared the number of dollops to the flatness of the Bundle.   There was nothing more to do today so she had been right in her dollop apportioning. She reminded herself that on some days she was given a lot of assistance from other people and that helped enormously.   On those days she would use the 'spare' Energy that she hadn't needed, to re-stock and pay back the Energy she had borrowed - so all in all and more or less her debit and credit Energy balance was pretty even.   (On days when the debit was too great there was very little she could do, and she had to stay in bed and wait for the Bundle to re-fill itself.)

Also, sometimes it was pleasant to waste Energy.   Just for the fun of it.   To spend it on something really different -

like going for an unnecessary walk, not to arrive anywhere but just to enjoy the walking. On those days it seemed that the Bundle grew fatter - as if she got more Energy back than she was spending . . . things were often very confusing and sometimes it is better not to think so hard about things as it may take more Energy in the thinking than is gained in the solutioning.

She frowned to herself. 'What is to be done?' she thought. 'Maybe the Wisdom of Years will help me to plan my use of Energy better. Or maybe not. Or maybe I just have to be grateful that no matter how much Energy I use, there is usually enough in the Bundle on the morrow.'

And there she was, thinking again, but now with very little Energy left in the Bundle she decided to give up and go to bed.

She had decisions to make and battles to fight and win, but that was all best left for another day.

Funny how we interpret things, thought the lady.

On Seeking a Way Out

The Hall

The Hour Glass

The worker ants were scurrying from here to there and back again in a desperate attempt to keep the levels up.

As they dropped the grains of sand into the Hour Glass they (the grains of sand) seemed to disappear almost immediately such was the demand.

Eric and Stanley sat down for a moment.

'I don't think I can keep this up,' said Eric.

'I feel the same, yet what choice have we?'

'You mean this is our lot in life?' Eric furrowed his brow and scratched his antennae.

'Yes, I suppose so,' replied Stanley. 'We were born worker ants and we shall die worker ants, as did our parents before us.'

'God that's depressing,' said Eric. 'So there's really no other future for us?'

'Other future? Well no not really, but what would you do if you were able to change your future? Gathering the sand is all we know.'

'Oh, I dunno,' said Eric. 'Live a little. Take up windsurfing . . . learn to play the tuba . . . stuff like that.'

'A worker ant playing the tuba,' scoffed Stanley good naturedly. 'Now that is something I would like to see.'

'You know what I mean Stan. I have dreams and I want to be able to realise them - I want to be able to teach my antling that if he applies himself he can achieve anything.'

'Y - e - s . . .'

'Stan,' said Eric standing tall (as tall as he could) and stretching his six little legs, 'wouldn't you like to break out, just once maybe and do something different . . . I dunno, see the lights - go to the city, maybe take in a show . . . to fly . . .'

'Your parents weren't flying ants Eric? Were they?'

'No no Stan, but you know what I mean. Monotony kills you know.'

Stanley was obviously struggling to keep up with Eric's flight of fancy.

'Eric, mate. We could have a couple of days off. We can requisition the time tomorrow, grab the girls and then take off for some fun and hilarity. That'll set you right.'

Eric grimaced (inwardly). This was not what he meant.

'Naaaeeeerrrr' the siren sounded.

'Sector Seven. This is not an authorised break. Continue with your work,' announced the gruff announcer.

'Come on mate,' said Stanley. 'We'd better keep going.'

* * *

A very long time ago when there were not so many humans and other creatures in the world, it had been a pleasant enough job to keep the Hour Glass topped up. More recently however the population had exploded, but not in a 'boufff gone forever' way. The population had exploded which meant that there were now many many many more humans and other creatures all demanding their share of time. Since the so called explosion it had taken much more effort, and time, to keep the Hour Glass filled - yet the workforce had not increased in number. There were indeed more humans and other creatures but very few extra ants. The demand made upon them was such that they did not have very much time to explode their own population.

(Historically worker ants were female, but a long time ago those who decided very important things realised that since the 'explosion' the work required to keep the Hour Glass full was far too important and rather too taxing to leave to the females, so they had had their roles reversed. In those far off days before the role reversal, the males were only ever seen when it was time to mate with the Queen, after which they died. Tough love. Interestingly the Queen, contrary to popular belief, had never been a tyrant. She did not sit around having her nails painted and sipping pink champagne. She was simply portrayed as such. The worker ants themselves had generally always decided which tasks needed doing around the colony. Since the roles of the ants had been reversed however, the Queen became the Wise One of the colony and lived in harmony with everyone else. And the males lived longer. And had their own families. And everyone was pretty happy.)

So the now male worker ants spent their days to-ing and fro-ing, collecting and delivering the Sands of Time, each following exactly the same route, as ants do, each avoiding exactly the same boulders or barricades on their path and each going slowly around the bend, as ants do. Every now and then an exhausted ant would lose his footing and drop into the Hour Glass and become lost in the sands. In the outside world this extra 'substance' created a rumbling kerplumph when that particular grain was used.

* * *

Later that day when the final siren sounded three times, Eric and Stanley wiped their hairy eyebrows, washed their mandibles in the water trough and knocked off for the day. They returned to their colony.

Eric and Stanley were best friends, brothers really, as were their wives (not brothers, best friends. Each other's that is).

'Hello boys, good day at the front?' asked Sadie, Eric's wife.

'Same old same old you know,' replied Eric.

June, Stanley's wife, brought out a couple of beers and a pot of potatoes. The menfolk were grateful for the beer and each took a long pull from their glass. They sat around, peeling the potatoes and chatting whilst their wives put the antlings to bed and discussed how they might spice up the leaves they had gathered during the day. Sadie had found some wonderful rotting nectarines in an empty house nearby and had managed to drag a sizeable amount home.

So today there was pudding.

June had climbed to the top of a wilting balsam and brought home some incredibly juicy black fruit flies. Yum.

There would indeed be a feast that evening.

'Eric mate, that stuff you were saying earlier.'

'Yes Stan?'

'Well, do you think it is really possible?'

'What do you mean Stan?'

'Do you think a worker ant can really break out, even just for a day?'

Eric was enjoying his beer, and he was enjoying the moment.

Eric really did have dreams.

Eric had decided long ago that the life of a worker ant was not for him, even though his father had been one and had lived a happy (so he had said) and fulfilled (so he had said) life.

'I do. All we need is a plan. And we need to give ourselves some time . . .'

And that was how it started. Eric and Stanley thought of little else for days.

Stanley, albeit that he had been slow at first to catch on, became obsessed with the idea of breaking out. Not for him the high life, the bright lights and the buzz of the city, nor did he wish to learn to play a musical instrument or discover the joys of Newquay. But he had a mathematical mind and had once dreamed of being a teacher ant. He thought, indeed he knew, that he had more to give than the to-ing and fro-ing of gathering the sands. Not that he knocked the job, it was work after all and it paid the bills. Most of his friends felt the same and were happy to do the job provided they had alternate Saturdays off.

* * *

The days passed in the to-ing and fro-ing.

Stanley continued to hatch his plan and Eric continued to dream. On some warm and starry nights Eric could be seen lying on his back outside his front door, gazing up to the heavens, puffing on a Havana. On the same starry nights Stanley would be at his desk, pencil and slide rule in mandible, working out a great many things. He worked out a great many things for quite a long time until the walls of his study were covered in equations.

The days were the same and the nights became the same for Stanley until one day, whilst chomping on their packed lunch during the authorised lunch break, Stanley nudged Eric.

'I've got it, Eric.'

'What the saucisson sec leftovers from last night? Me too Stan.'

'No, Eric. No. A plan.'

'A plan?'

A plan. The plan.'

'A plan, the plan?'

'The plan Eric, THE plan.'

'The plan Stan? THE plan?'

'THE plan.'

'What plan?'

'The plan to end all plans. The plan you have been waiting for. The plan we have both been waiting for. THE plan.'

'THE plan?'

'Yes Eric. THE plan. The plan which will take us away from all of this.'

'You mean?'

'Yes, Eric. Freedom.'

Eric chocked on his saucisson.

'Blimey Stan, you are an ant with a plan?'

'I am Eric. I am an ant with a plan. I am an ant with THE plan. The answer.'

'Blimey. A plan, sorry THE plan which is also an answer. Is this some sort of crossword puzzle Stan?'

'No Eric. I am deadly serious.'

'Naaaeeeerrrr,' the siren sounded.

'Too much talking in Sector Seven. Continue with your work,' announced the gruff announcer.

(Eric and Stanley had never seen the gruff announcer. They did not know if he were ant or human or any other creature. They would, on several occasions, have dearly liked to knee him in whatever parts he had.)

They got up and brushed the crumbs from their tabards.

(The tabard had been introduced for the younger workers who sometimes, for showing off reasons, tried to carry too many grains at a time or, heaven forfend, juggle with them. This latter act caused much frowning amongst the older, wiser workers. (Should the gruff announcer spot such irresponsible behaviour there would, they all knew, be hell to pay. One worker had been caught, ordered out of the line, and was never seen again. But that didn't stop the young ones from larking about. The recklessness of youth, eh?) The tabard had a pocket, à la kangaroo, so that should any of the precious grains drop they would most probably slide into the tabard pocket where they could be picked out by the workers and not stick to their hot little exoskeletons or, double heaven forfend, be lost forever.)

'See you at yours after work. I will tell you everything,' said Stanley mysteriously, winking.

When the final siren sounded three times and after the mandatory mandible rinse, Eric and Stanley trudged the long road home to the colony. Trudged yes, but with a lighter step than usual. Stan had a plan to divulge and they were both excited.

Sadie brought out the beer.

'Thank you my love,' said Eric.

'Anything to do? Potatoes?' asked Stanley.

'No you're alright,' replied Sadie. 'June and I have it all under control. You boys sit there and chew over the fat.' (She did not bring out a bag of pork scratchings, this was just a saying.)

Sadie went inside and she and June washed the little ones and prepared to read them a bedtime story.

'Right,' said Eric. 'Spill the beans. What's the plan Stan?'

'Okay Eric. I have worked out with my equations and my slide rule that we can break out. Get away from all of this and take our wives and antlings with us.'

'Yes, right, well, that was the general idea,' replied Eric, so far non-plussed.

'Ah yes, but how to do it Eric, hmm?'

'Well, we pack our bags and do a runner.'

'Were it that simple we, or at least you, would have done it ages ago. Think Eric. Think.'

'Well come on Stan with the plan, tell me.'

Stanley took a deep sip of beer and a deep breath. He felt on the verge of greatness.

'Okay Eric. You said something the other day. About giving ourselves some time, and that is what I propose we do.'

Stanley explained that if they could give themselves some time they would be able to make their escape undetected. If they gave themselves enough time they could start afresh and then tap into the Hour Glass from elsewhere. But they would have to be very clever and extremely cautious.

'And we tell no-one,' said Stanley. 'No-one.'

'And how do you propose that we give ourselves some time?' asked Eric.

'Right. This is where it becomes interesting. We take it. We take time. We take Time.'

'Eh?' now it was Eric who was being slow.

Eric was a great friend and father. He was a great husband. He was a great dreamer and thinker. But he was not practical. Not in the slightest. He was more of a poet really.

'Right. Here is the equation.' Stanley produced a small piece of paper from inside his exoskeleton.

'What, that's it?' asked Eric. 'Several weeks of planning and this small piece of paper is the result?'

'Yes Eric. I have condensed the equation into the important bit. How I arrived at the important bit would take too long to explain and I do not have a piece of paper large enough to write it on. Besides which it is rather complicated.'

Stanley uncrumpled the piece of paper carefully and showed it to Eric.

On the piece of paper was written:

$4 \times 22 + 3 \times 19 + 10$ (in case) $= 155$

Stanley looked extremely pleased with himself.

'155?' said Eric.

'Yes.'

'155 what?'

'Grains of sand Eric. 155 grains of sand.'

'Sorry?'

'155 grains of sand is the time it will take us to get far enough away to be unknown where we end up.'

'R-i-g-h-t . . .'

'So we take the Time we need. No more no less. Apart from the extra 10 grains for 'just in case'.'

'Slow down, slow down, slow down Stan. You mean this is the plan?'

'Yes.'

'THE plan?'

'Yes.'

'THE plan Stan?'

'Yes. Eric. This is the plan. This is THE plan. It will work.'

Stanley explained the equation to Eric. There were four adults and three antlings. The antlings required fewer grains than the adults as they were smaller and they slept more. The 155 grains would buy them all 6 days to make their getaway and wind up elsewhere. 6.9047619047619 days to be precise. With 10 left over. Hopefully. 10 left over would give them just enough time to link in to the Hour Glass from the elsewhere.

Eric looked a little shocked. He looked as though he had been swatted with a feather duster. Not hurt just baffled.

'Eric, trust me,' said Stanley.

June and Sadie were chatting away inside and supper was nearly ready.

'Meet me behind the bike shed an hour after supper and I will tell you how we will do it,' said Stanley.

An hour after supper Eric and Stanley sat behind the bike shed.

Stanley explained to Eric that if they took only the small grains they would be able to smuggle them out without drawing attention to themselves.

'But this has never been done before,' said Eric.

'No Eric, and that is precisely why it will work. No one will be expecting or suspecting that such a thing might happen.'

'And how are we going to smuggle the grains out? In our tabards?'

'No Eric. Too obvious.'

'So?'

'So. We will select a small grain each day and pop it in our metasomas.'

(Since ants these days were very busy to-ing and fro-ing they rarely needed their poison sacks to poison anything, therefore their metasomas were largely redundant and had become small and rather withered.)

'I see . . . I see . . .' said Eric.

'And then we will store the grains in my study and when we have enough Pouff. Outta here.'

'R-i-g-h-t . . .' said Eric.

'77 shifts Eric. That is all it will take. 77 shifts.'

'And then?'

'Then?'

'Yes, then. How do we escape?'

'Ahah.'

Stanley was very proud of this next bit.

'Tiger Moth.'

'Eh?'

'Tiger Moth. One of the last training moths. Been in service since the great days.'

'Tiger Moth?'

'Yes Eric. There is one who lives not far from here. I have already had a word. He says he would love to take us. He has the perfect wingspan and hasn't had a decent flight in ages.'

Eric and Stanley looked at each other. Eric had finally and totally caught on. Eric was just beginning to realise that his hopes and dreams could become a reality.

'And we can't tell the girls?'

'No. Too dangerous for them.'

It was late and Eric and Stanley went home to their beds. They needed some sleep - which of course neither of them managed as they were far too excited.

The next morning it began.

Slowly, slowly and cautiously, they took one small grain each shift and popped it into their metasomas, and although they felt incredibly self conscious to begin with (Stanley blushed so much that he felt sure someone would notice) they became rather adept at the procedure.

Over the next few days they took their prized grains and walked (not ran) to Stanley's study before joining the girls for the evening.

Until.

Freedom was in sight.

The day was approaching.

The Tiger Moth was primed.

The grains of sand were in the bag.

Eric and Stanley had packed the essentials into small suitcases.

On the 70th shift there was one dodgy moment when Stanley stumbled along the path to the exit and almost dropped his grain.

'Naaaeeeerrrr,' the siren sounded. (Honestly, where was this guy?) 'Workers who are not up to the task will be relieved of their duties,' announced the gruff announcer.

Stanley steadied himself and walked out through the gate.

'Relieved?' said Stanley, and they both shuddered.

'This is it then,' said Eric to Stanley as they chopped the curly kale.

'In two days we fly.'

'Yes Eric. In two days we fly.'

They blinked triumphantly through their eyebrows.

* * *

The glorious day arrived. Eric and Stanley knew that it was a day not without danger.

'Goodbye doll,' said Eric to Sadie as he left for the day. 'I love you, you know.'

'And I love you too sweet pea,' replied Sadie.

'You do trust me, don't you Sadie?'

'Of course sweetest love. Why?'

'Oh no reason. Tell you what Sadie, don't make supper tonight. Stan and I are going to take you girls and the antlings out for grub.'

'Oooh Eric, how exciting. Now, what shall I wear . . .'

And Sadie pottered off to work out her wardrobe, suspecting nothing more than an evening out.

It was the same at Stanley's house.

'Now my dear. I hope you have a pleasant day and I will see you later.'

'Yes Stanley.'

'And my dear June, I do love you.'

'And I love you too Stanley.'

'And June, you do trust me?'

'Yes Stanley.'

'In all things?'

'Yes of course Stanley. Why?'

'Because things are not always what they seem June.'

'Pard'n?'

'Oh don't mind me. But you know I shall always love you and will and would only ever do the right thing by you and the antlings.'

'Yes Stanley. You are worrying me now . . .'

Stanley quickly wiped a tiny tear from his eye. Demonstrations of strong emotions always affected him deeply. There was a lot of the poet in him too.

'Goodbye my dear. Until this evening. Eric and I are taking you and the antlings out for supper so be ready.'

And with that he strode out of the house.

Stan was not only an ant with a plan he was also an ant on a mission.

The two friends worked their shift almost silently. They could feel the seriousness of the situation. They knew that this was it. This was the day. This was make or break. Break out or perish in the attempt.

Gathering the last of the smallest grains of sand and popping them into their metasomas, they left.

They left silently.

They left without a backward glance.

They did not say 'whoop whoop' and they did not dance along the track which led to their homes.

They walked in silence.

As they rounded the final bend they stopped.

Stanley put his claw on Eric's feeler.

Surreptitiously Eric handed Stanley his last grain.

'See you in ten.'

'See you in ten Eric.'

'Stan?'

'Yes Eric?'

'I love you mate.'

The two friends went each to their own homes.

The girls were ready.

The antlings were ready.

Stanley and June stepped out of their house, the antlings following behind.

A particularly large Tiger Moth taxied into the garden.

'What on earth?' said June.

'No time to explain, come on June, antlings. Hop aboard. June, trust me,' and Stanley grabbed his wife's claw and helped them all aboard.

Eric did the same with Sadie and their antling.

The Tiger Moth spread his wings and rose above the garden. He did a quick circle above the colony and then flew off in the direction of elsewhere.

* * *

Back at the Hour Glass no-one noticed that they or the sand were missing. And Time did not run out.

Smiling, the lady determined that she would access her inner ant and find her own way out.

'Get some help' the brother had said.

The Myna

The Elf went to the Town Hall. She needed some help as there was nothing left in her bundle and for breakfast that day she had eaten bluegreen coloured bread, which was not normal.

She sat in line waiting her turn and thought she might be a little scared of the Myna behind the desk who had a frownyface. The Myna was peering over her glasses at the human in front of her. The human talked, the Myna frowned.

The Myna then both talked and frowned. The human talked again and the Myna frowned again. The Myna shook her head and the human left.

The Myna signalled to the Elf.

'Miss Elf?'

The Elf went forward and sat in front of the Myna.

'Now then what can I do for you?' she asked.

'Well I really could do with a bit of help from you, er, please,' replied the Elf.

'Yes my dear but in what way? What is going on with you?' asked the Myna.

'Um, well, it's just that I seem to have run out of most things and I am struggling a bit.'

'My dear Miss Elf,' said the Myna removing her spectacles. 'Tell me all about it.'

The Elf started to tell the Myna all about it. How one day things had started to go wrong. How she had been told by the Men on the Outside that everything was to become more expensive, but that she would have to pay. How a particular human had not been telling the truth. How she had been let down by many humans and other creatures and how she had been stuck in a Waiting Room for a very long time with nothing much happening. And how her dreams of starting her own little shop had been dashed when the Decision Makers at the bank had not even considered her request as it had been a request at the end of a long line of requests, apparently, which had fallen off the end of the long line of requests when the bank had finally collapsed. (She left out the bit about confronting Mr Swestern, the Bank Manager, as she didn't want to come across as a trouble maker. She also left out the bit about having started a small revolution for the same reason.) She told the Myna that now she was running out of Energy and couldn't seem to quite manage on her own.

All this time the Myna listened carefully and neither shook her head nor tutted. And she didn't frown at all. Not once.

When the Elf had finished her story the Myna got up, crossed the room, picked up two glasses of sweet juice and returned to her desk. She smiled at the Elf.

The Myna was really nice and although she had a frownyface she didn't show it to the Elf as the Elf was simply telling the truth. (The Myna only showed the frownyface to humans and other creatures who needed to see it.) The Myna was a beautiful bird and while they were drinking their sweet juice she showed her wonderful gold and red and steel blueness - her true colours.

(Fact. Myna birds do not have gold, red and steely blue iridescent feathers, but this particular Myna's father was a Royal Starling, who had not only given her her true colours, but also her somewhat haughty demeanour.)

They talked a lot more and the Elf left with a list of things to do, promising to return in two weeks.

The Elf continued to attend the Town Hall every two weeks and would sit patiently awaiting her turn, observing the others around her but trying not to stare. Whilst waiting for the Myna she started writing notes about the humans and other creatures who were also waiting to be seen. Gradually over the following weeks she became aware of the air in the room deflating slightly.

On one particular visit the Elf had been reduced to tears when the Myna told her that all the efforts she had put in 'did not count.' Nothing counted. The next time they talked more about the Elf's attempts at getting herself out of *the difficult situation, but this time the Elf said to the Myna 'I have done this, this and this,' (showing the Myna a long list) 'but I have not kept a record of the other things I have done as you said they did not count.'*

'But you must record each and everything you do,' replied the Myna.

'But why when you said that some of my attempts do not count? What is the point of recording those?'

'No Miss Elf. You must record everything, even though it may not count, and you must try to find a proper solution.'

'Well there you are. You have just used the word 'proper' which underlines your total disregard of all my other efforts, and I shall therefore not record them as, according to you, they are not proper and they do not count.'

That time when the Elf left, the plumage on the Myna's head appeared rather less iridescent.

There followed many such visits. On another occasion the Myna appeared a little flustered. At the adjacent desk another bird, not as beautiful as the Myna, was interviewing a small human. The Myna looked across and interjected into their conversation.

'No no Geoffrey. That is not what we said last week.' And then, back to the Elf. 'Now where are you Miss Elf, I cannot find you in my records.'

'Well I am right here, at the right time on the right day,' the Elf replied.

'Yes, but you are not in my box and therefore I cannot record our meeting.' The Myna looked over to Geoffrey again.

'Geoffrey, you will have to see the others downstairs. You will have to wait for them to be able to talk to you, which

might take a very long time indeed, and you must sort this out.'

Back to the Elf. 'Now, where are you, where are you?'

The Elf couldn't help thinking that if only the Myna concentrated fully on either Geoffrey or finding her in the box, one of the issues would have been sorted more effectively.

Geoffrey got up to leave saying 'Oh well. There you are. It is a member of my family who has made this mistake, dropped me in it and caused all this trouble.' And he left.

'That is his mistake,' said the Elf to the Myna. 'He is blaming someone else for something which is his responsibility. He needs to get a grip.' The Myna smiled. 'Exactly, Miss Elf. Now where are you?'

The weeks went on and the Elf grew to recognise more of the humans and other creatures who also attended the Town Hall fortnightly. And she noticed that slowly things were changing. Same crowd, same place. But. The shoulders drooped a little more each time. The gait became less swaggery. The pallor started blurring at the edges and the overall demeanour of the folk became dowdier with each visit.

The Myna and others who sat behind the desks did their best. They asked the right questions and, with their long beaks, they tried to sniff out the Wrongdoers. With humans and other creatures who were telling the truth they smiled and nodded and offered Good Advice. But you can't force things to happen if they are not going to happen and sometimes the humans and other creatures wept a little and asked the unanswerable question, Why? Neither the Myna nor her colleagues could answer that one. But they uttered kind words such as 'I am sure you will find something soon.' But the Elf and others started not to believe this. And yet they must. They had to believe something or they would lose HOPE - and without hope the dark door of Nothingness would open.

They had all heard the door open - a yawning, groaning, guttural sound it makes as the Zombie Keeper of the Door beckons to those who are ready to cross the threshold and enter the eternal numb.

One day it nearly happened. The Elf noticed someone teetering dangerously close to the edge. The human turned, momentarily, towards the room. 'Noooooooooo' the Elf cried and, caught as she was in the slow-motion-running scenario which occurs when things are very important, she glimpsed something she recognised deep within the human's psyche. It was herself, or rather a shadow of herself, printed like a smudgy litho against the human's own smudge. A shadowy smudge of the solidarity of hopelessness, barely perceptible yet irrefutably there. And then she realised . . . the human was Geoffrey!

'No Geoffrey Noooo . . .' her outer self screamed - she had to help Geoffrey or they would all be lost.

'Come back Geoffrey, come back. There is always Hope.'

'Too late. No Hope left,' replied Geoffrey, still struggling to decide which direction he should take.

'No,' said the Elf grabbing Geoffrey's arm. 'You are wrong. Let's go for a cuppa and see if we can find Hope again for you.'

Geoffrey turned slowly, shuffled away from the threshold and left the Town Hall with the Elf. The Zombie

Keeper of the Door simply closed the door, confident in the knowledge that he would re-open it again soon enough.

* * *

The next time the Myna asked the Elf what skills she possessed.

'Well. I can knit hats for small insects. I can bake very fine cakes and I am good at mending things. I can decorate windows, tell good stories and translate from the French.'

The Myna told the Elf that she would have to broaden her options and attend a course on 'how to be more interesting to the executive employment market.' (Eh?) She showed the Elf some information about the course (which contained lots of words which made no sense whatsoever to the Elf) and made a date for the Elf to attend. But the course was due to take place during a time when the Elf's Hermit Mother and Little Lily were coming to stay, and they would all be together.

'I cannot attend this course Miss Myna. Please can you offer me an alternative?'

'No Miss Elf. You must attend this one.'

'But my Hermit Elf Mother and Little Lily are coming to stay and it will be the first time for months that we will all be together.'

'That does not matter. You must attend the course,' reiterated the Myna, with a slight wince.

'But that is unreasonable. Surely there must be some leeway for occasions such as these?'

'Well Miss Elf. You can write down all your reasons for not being able to attend the course and I will give your reasons to the Decision Makers.'

BONGGGGGGG. The memory of dealing with such humans before made the Elf feel rather jagged.

'After all,' continued the Myna. 'Rules is Rules'.'

'But how can we live within such rules?' said the Elf.

'Well,' said the Myna, now not wincing but frowning. 'You do what we say and, when the time comes, we will ring the bell when you secure a job . . .' and all along the Elf had clapped, honestly, for the humans and other creatures who had secured jobs. But that day she stopped clapping. In fact she stopped completely.

'Miss Myna. You will not secure me a job for I am not conventionally employable and I cannot be someone I am not. It is not your fault but, Miss Myna, I am out of here.'

And with that the Elf delved into her bundle, brought out a bell, and rang it. Loudly. For herself. She rang her own bell and then she left.

Ask not for whom the bell tolls . . .

The lady thought about kindness, not because she found others unkind, but at times she felt that they were not necessarily kind in the way she needed them to be (which in itself might be an unkind thought she wondered . . . you see?)

The Inner Hall

DAYWBDB

(or for those of you who have forgotten your Charles Kingsley, Do As You Would Be Done By.)

Omar looked up at the sky.

It was big, as big as it should be, but something was wrong. He scratched his head.

What was it? What was it? And then he realised. No stars. There were no stars.

* * *

Omar lived in IndiaLand. He was very happy and spent his days helping the visitors. The visitors wanted to experience the real IndiaLand and asked many questions. They were usually nice humans and were mostly neither rude nor shouty. Omar served them well.

Omar became particularly fond of a group of visitors who came in the January month. And they became particularly fond of him. It was a reciprocated pleasure for each to be in the other's company. Omar looked after the visitors well, and even though they didn't always understand what he was saying he was so very nice that they were sure that whatever it was he was saying would be lovely, so they smiled and nodded and thanked him - for all and everything.

The visitors told Omar a little of their country and Omar became curious. Over time Omar's curiosity grew and grew, and when he had saved enough money from the generous tips the visitors pressed upon him he booked a seat on an aeroplane.

(In IndiaLand it was considered normal to give tips based on a daily rate, and visitors were encouraged to leave their tip - should they wish to give one - on their beds on the day they were leaving. This way, so the guide books informed, the tips would be shared between all those who had helped to make the visitors' stay enjoyable. Between all, seen and unseen, for as we know it is not simply whoever cleans the room whom we might wish to thank, but also those who help to wash the vegetables and those who sweep the grass outside each day. Sometimes if a group of visitors felt especially grateful to a particular somebody, they would break the rules and press a crisp fiver on that particular somebody - and as Omar was genuinely very lovely he often found himself with a handful of crisp fivers. He would smile inwardly and then he would not go out drinking the stuff which made some of the visitors fall over. No. He would take his crisp fivers home and at the end of each month he would deposit them in the bank. It was in this way that Omar managed to save enough to buy his aeroplane ticket to the FarawayLand.)

* * *

So Omar had discovered that there were no stars in the skies above Old London Town.

(The truth is of course that there are stars in the skies above Old London Town, but there is also a great deal of light pollution which not only makes the skies look dull and cloudy on most evenings but also totally obliterates the stars. So even though they are there, twinkling away for all their might, the humans who live in Old London Town are quite unaware of the fact. This sad lack of star sighting is okay for the older humans who have visited FarawayLands as they knew the facts, but it was rather a shame for the children who, not having had much travel experience, were quite unaware of the wonders they were missing.)

As well as no stars in the skies there were also no cows in the roads. Back in IndiaLand there were always cows in the roads and everyone made way for them. Humans walked around the cows or let them pass first. No one minded and no one became cross and blared their horns or shouted 'Hey you. Fatty. Get outta the way.' Or 'Shift it, sister.' Nothing like that. In Omar's country the cow was a sacred beast and always in the right.

* * *

Omar also discovered that in Old London Town folk seemed to get very cross a lot of the time. They shouted or tutted or said 'Grrrrh'. Back in IndiaLand things could certainly be exasperating, yet the overall mood was one of patience, acceptance and understanding. Of trying to do the right thing at any given moment and being considerate of others. Oh, and also that to do something kind was as pleasurable for the he or she who had done the kind thing as for the he or she who had had the kind thing done to or for them.

In Old London Town however Omar heard many folk ask 'What's in it for me?' before they didn't do whatever was being asked of them.

Omar found this disconcerting and was saddened that most of the folk he met along the way didn't understand how much better, lighter and more joyous you feel if you do something kind, simply because you can.

One day he offered to help someone carry his heavy suitcase to the bus.

'Clear off,' said the someone.

'Let me help you,' said Omar (whose English had improved somewhat since the January month).

'Buzz off. There's nothing for you 'ere,' said the someone, struggling with his case.

'But I can help you,' repeated Omar.

'Why? Wassinit for you?' said the someone.

'What do you mean?' asked Omar.

'No one does nuffing for nuffing,' said the someone (which was a little confusing for Omar who was not used to the double negative).

'You need help, and I can help,' said Omar, smiling. 'I want nothing for myself.'

'Clear off, you foreign . . .' said the someone, and so much did he struggle to get his suitcase onto the bus that he fell from the step and his case flew open, spilling its insides out.

'Now look what you made me do,' snarled the someone.

Omar wondered why he was responsible for this misfortune. He bent down and started helping the someone to gather his belongings.

'Where you from then,' asked the someone.

'I am from IndiaLand,' replied Omar.

'Hmm . . . that's where we 'ave our call centres,' replied the someone.

'Yes. Many of my friends work in your call centres,' replied Omar.

'Yea, and every time we get redirected to a call centre in your land we sigh and grimace and say bleedin' 'ell,' said the someone.

'I am aware of that,' said Omar. 'My friends say that many of your fellow Englanders are not at all kind.'

'That's because you can't bleedin' speak English,' said the someone.

'But I think the people who work in the call centres work there because they *can* speak English,' said Omar.

'Well, wha'ever . . . an' it always takes so bleedin' long to get answers to our questions.'

'But that may not be the fault of the human at the other end of the phone,' said Omar. 'Maybe it is a problem with the companies who employ the humans in the call centres.'

'Pffw,' said the someone.

Strewn stuff gathered, the someone stood back to wait for the next bus.

'Actually, many of the humans who phone the call centres are very rude,' said Omar. 'Some of my friends go home from work feeling very sad.'

'Shouldn't do the job then,' said the someone.

'Why? Why is it not a problem with your humans? Why should they be so rude?'

'Brrrrggghh,' said the someone. 'They get paid for it, don't they.'

'They do, but not very much. And there is a certain place in my land where the young girls work very hard making clothing for your ladies and gentlemen, and they get paid very little too.'

'Shouldn't do the work then.'

Omar realised that although his English had improved greatly since the January month, he was going to be unable to argue the pros and cons of what he knew was sweated labour with this someone. He simply didn't have the vocabulary.

He bid the someone goodbye.

'Any 'ow,' continued the someone. ''Ow come you wanted to 'elp me?'

'Don't you have an expression in your country which says something like "Do as you would be done by"?'

'Blimey,' said the someone.

'In my land we live by a creed which encourages us to help our fellow man whenever we can, to try to see the positive and to spread joy wherever we go.' (He was rather proud of that last sentence.)

'You sound like a right bible puncher.' said the someone. 'You religious types. Honestly. Ge' a life.'

Omar thought about this and then, in the very best English he could find in his brain, he said 'I am not a bible puncher - I do not speak of religion - the way of life we have in my land is a very big way of life. We just believe in the inherent goodness in all.'

'Blimey,' said the someone, who wasn't quite sure if he understood.

'Goodbye,' said Omar.

'Pfffffrrrr,' said the someone.

* * *

That evening in the pub the someone was telling his friend about the strange stranger he had met that day.

'Goin' round doin' good,' he said. 'Funny way to go about stuff.'

'Yea, coming over 'ere and not speaking the language.' said his friend.

The someone did not tell his friend that in fact Omar had a very good command of the language, so much so that he himself was not sure he had understood all that Omar had said.

'Yea . . .'

* * *

Omar went back to his lodgings, thinking all the while. He thought about his Aunty who swept the grass outside one of the big hotels so that the grass always looked perfect. All the humans who worked in the big hotels wanted to make sure that the visitors who came to stay had the very best of times. This sentiment was not restricted to the hotel workers. All the humans the visitors met on their stay in IndiaLand wanted to make sure that the visitors had the very best of times. And it was genuine. And they did not do all they did in order to get money. They did all they did because they could.

Omar turned the final corner before arriving back at his lodgings. It was dark. And cold.

He put his key in the lock and opened the door.

'That you Omar?' came a voice from the kitchen.

'Oh hello Polly, yes, Omar here.'

'Come on in Omar.'

Omar opened the kitchen door and there was Polly, all smiles. She was wearing an apron and was mostly covered in flour.

'How was your day Omar? Been anywhere nice?'

'Just around Polly. Learning more about your country.'

'Cuppa?' said Polly.

'Great.'

And Polly made a pot of tea and she and Omar chatted about this and that - mostly that. Polly pushed a plate of ginger biscuits under Omar's nose.

'I've been baking, have one . . . or four,' she said.

Omar took a biscuit. They were good. He reached for another one.

'Tell you what Omar, let me make you up a plate. You can take it up to your room and nibble any time you like.'

Polly lifted a meat platter down from the dresser and started to fill it with biscuits and cakes and all sorts of tasty bits and bobs.

'Thank you Polly, you are so kind,' beamed Omar as he took the platter from her.

'Not kind Omar. It gives me pleasure to see you wolfing down my biscuits. Got no one to cook for now.'

* * *

Omar went up the stairs bearing his gifts and smiling broadly.

Polly closed the kitchen door and dusted herself down. She picked up a favourite cook book. 'Now what shall I cook tomorrow,' she wondered, smiling broadly.

* * *

The next day Omar went out and about along the river which travels through the city. He walked a very long way and was surprised by the enormously different dwelling houses on the riverbank. Some houses were very grand and resembled palaces, whilst others were similar to the tin huts of the shantytowns on the outskirts of the city in which he lived.

Omar had brought some of his leftover biscuits and cakes with him, and feeling peckish he sat down by the river and pulled out his little bag.

Then it happened.

BANGGGGGG

BOOOOOFFFF

Something or someone crashed into Omar, biffed him over the head with something blunt, rifled through his pockets for his wallet, found it, took it, and legged it.

'Nooo noooo,' yelled Omar as the something or someone raced away.

No good. The something or someone disappeared and Omar struggled to sit up. His head hurt. His head hurt and his spirit hurt.

There wasn't very much money in Omar's wallet, but it wasn't that which upset him. Omar carried little photographs of his family in the wallet and he suddenly felt terribly alone. He felt alone in a strange land and he very much wanted to go home.

'Come on Son,' said a voice.

Omar squinted up from where he sprawled, and there was the someone from the previous day. The someone who had not let Omar help him and whose suitcase had burst.

'Come on, Son, gis yer 'and,' said the someone who, in a gentler way than his manner might suggest, took Omar's hand and helped him to sit up properly.

'You look a right mess. Wot 'appened?'

Omar told his sorry tale and together they shared the leftover biscuits.

'Thank you for your kindness,' said Omar.

'Hrrrmph,' said the someone.

'What was in in for you?' asked Omar.

'Nuffing,' said the someone. 'But you know what, I feel good.'

* * *

It is the last evening.

Omar is getting ready to leave tomorrow.

Polly calls up the stairs.

'Omar, will you come to the kitchen later? I have something for you.'

Omar finished packing up his belongings and went downstairs. The smells coming from the kitchen were amazing. It smelled a little like home. His home.

Polly had made Tikka Masala.

It tasted great.

'Thank you Polly, that was delicious.'

'Omar, it has been my pleasure to have you stay with me . . . will you come again to Old London Town?'

'Yes Polly, I shall. And Polly?'

'Yes Omar?'

'Will you come to stay with me in IndiaLand?'

'Yes Omar, I shall.'

And Yet More Help Required
The Enforcement Officer

The Elf had a sinking feeling. Deep in her tummy. A deep sinking feeling.

Blast.

She would have to contact the Town Hall (again) regarding a certain something that had occurred in her new little house. Not in her new little house but next to her new little house. And seeping over her new little house. The Elf's sinking feeling was due to the memory of having to contact such folk before - folk such as The Myna and The Bankleys Bank crowd.

The Elf had no desire to make waves but the something that had happened was rather important. Not only important but potentially damaging.

To her house.

And to humans and other creatures.

And to peaceful tranquil living.

The Elf girded her loins and put on her armour (her favourite wellington boots) and made the call. The Human at the Town Hall was very nice. '4pm on a Friday?' he had said. 'Yes, 4pm on a Friday yet you are still there and I have quite a simple question for you.'

'Only joking,' (which was a rare thing for anyone at the Town Hall to say as they didn't often joke, let alone find anything amusing if humans or other creatures dared to do so themselves).

The Human at the Town Hall was called Mr Darling Darling and he was very nice and, it turned out, very knowledgeable. He listened to the Elf's questions and then said 'I will report this to The Enforcement Officer. He will contact you within two weeks.'

They bid each other a cheery goodbye and the Elf had a think.

The Enforcement Officer.

That sounded rather dark.

Rather like the baddies in the films she had watched with her little daughter.

Enter The Enforcement Officer.

Da Da Daaaahhhhhhh . . .

The Elf, and humans and other creatures who lived close to her, had put up with quite a lot of jiggery pokery concerning and surrounding the house next door. They had put up with noise and more noise. They had put up with dust. They had put up with orange dust. Dust clouds of the sort of orange dust that are only created when someone has done something rather big. And blow they do, these dust clouds, and cover everything with their orangeyness. And they had put up with the bang bang bang and the drrrrh drrrrh drrrrh but sometimes they wept and couldn't sleep and wanted it all to stop.

'Please please can you stop - especially at night time and on days of rest?' they had asked the humans who were making the bang bang bang and the drrrrh drrrrh drrrrh noises.

And they did stop, a little.

But generally life went on like that. With a lot of noise and a growing bag of sad and bad feeling. It continued to be very noisy. There was barely any peace.

Barely any peace.

Very little peace.

Almost no peace.

None.

The humans and other creatures living close to the bang bang bang and the drrrrh drrrrh drrrrh noises tried to comfort themselves, saying in their brains and thinking and believing that 'one day this will all be over.'

Until.

Until.

Until.

A very big building was built on top of the house that emitted the bang bang bang and the drrrrh drrrrh drrrrh noises.

A really very big building.

A massive box type building that was rather ugly.

Because it was so big.

It towered above the little houses below it saying 'look at me, look at me, ha!'

That was one thing, but then the humans and other creatures who lived akin to this very big building noticed that quite apart from it being very big, it sat ON their houses.

Sorry?

What?

Pardon?

And that is why the Elf had ended up speaking with Mr Darling Darling. She had kept it brief. No needless chit chat. No name slinging or slanging.

'Can they do that?' she had asked.

'No Miss Elf.'

'So if they want to build a very big box building on top of their house, they should maybe have mentioned it to me first?'

'Yes Miss Elf.'

'And to the humans and other creatures who live on the other side of them?'

'Yes Miss Elf.'

'And to the humans and other creatures who live in this road?'

'Yes Miss Elf.'

'For example by putting up some sort of Notice on a tree or something? Quite apart from coming and telling us all?'

'Yes Miss Elf.'

'And, forgive me Darling Darling, if they decide they want to build a very big box building on top of their house

and decide not to speak to any one of us about it, should it sit a bit on my house?'

'No Miss Elf.'

And this is how it all started . . .

The Elf had visions of The Enforcement Officer arriving, clad in black leather and brandishing a machete. In reality he was a very nice gentleman human who did not resemble a Darth Vader character. He had seen more cases such as these than the noisy humans had most probably had hot dinners.

'You cannot keep that box building on your house,' he had told them. 'It is too big.'

'Oh yes we can,' they had replied, 'and there is nothing you can do about it.'

This was of course a very odd thing for someone to say to an enforcement officer, as being the Enforcement Officer it is his job is to make sure that humans and other creatures stick to the rules.

The Enforcement Officer told the noisy wrong humans that they would have to submit an application to him and he would decide what he was going to do with the very big box building. He also told them that if they simply applied to keep the very big box building the size it is, he would tell them to take it down.

Nothing happened.

The noisy wrong humans did not submit an application. They did not submit a simple application let alone one in triplicate.

There was going to be a long hard battle but the Elf felt that the Enforcement Officer would Do the Right Thing and that the noisy wrong humans would eventually have to do as they were told.

The story continues.

To deal again with the establishment - it made the lady tired just thinking about it . . .

What Curiosities we Appear to Need
The Sitting Room
The Value of Fluffles

'Stop,' cried the older member from the Peakington District. 'We cannot proceed. I am missing my ceremonial cloak. I cannot think without my fluffles.'

The members stopped. In their tracks. This interruption was a little unusual.

'When did you last have it dear?' asked Maurice, the older member from the Peakington District's oldest colleague and friend.

'Last month, when we were debating the value of reversing the way the aardvarks search for ants. When we decided that they would do less harm to the forest floor if they searched in an anti-clockwise direction, and . . .'

'Yes yes dear, and where did you put the cloak?'

'In the usual place, I thought . . .'

'But now it is not there?'

'No.'

Frowns all round.

'Has anyone seen his fluffles?' Maurice called out.

The other Keepers looked at each other.

'Um, no. No, we have not seen his fluffles . . . Not since, now, when was it,' pondered Dennis. 'I think we were debating the viability of wind farms on the deeply secluded island of Bryher.'

'Were we not debating the perils of introducing a law regarding the number of ostriches that can be kept in any one pen?'

'Cucumbers,' interrupted Cuthbert.

'Eh?'

'The last time I remember seeing his fluffles was when we were debating the optimum length of a cucumber.'

'Members please,' interrupted Maurice. 'This is a very serious situation. We cannot possibly proceed with today's debate until Octavia has his fluffles.'

The Keepers of The Laws led a very strange life and as they grew older some of them found comfort in talismans. Some of them found comfort in rituals, others found comfort in brandy. Most, on entering the House of Debate, would don their cloaks and wigs and ceremonial sashes. Octavia donned his fluffles. Octavia always donned his fluffles. Octavia was lost without his fluffles. Octavia would not go on without his fluffles.

(You may be thinking that Octavia is a strange name for a male member, but is it any stranger than Vivian I would ask.)

The Keepers of The Laws looked at each other. They were not quite sure what to do. They were not normally called upon to solve mysteries.

'How can we solve this mystery,' asked Maurice. 'Does anyone have any ideas?'

No one said anything.

'Can anyone suggest how we might locate the missing fluffles?' Maurice continued.

The Keepers of The Laws were not used to having ideas, and they were most certainly not used to coming up with solutions to problems.

(Most of the Keepers lived in rooms in the House of Debate where others had ideas and did things. Things such as cleaning and cooking and finding solutions to problems. Some of the Keepers lived in houses with their wives, but there too others did things.)

The Keepers looked at Maurice.

'What can we do?' they asked.

'We must systematically search the dressing rooms.'

'We?'

'Yes, we must systematically search the dressing rooms.'

'We?'

'Yes, ahem. We must systematically search the dressing rooms.'

'We?'

'Yes, we . . .'

'No, we mean we? We mean we? *We* must systematically search the dressing rooms?'

'Yes, we. We.'

'We?'

'Yes, we. Do you have a problem with that as a plan?'

The Keepers pushed Dennis forward, motioning to him that he should be the spokeskeeper.

'Um Maurice,' started Dennis. 'What some of the Keepers mean by 'we', I believe, is do you mean that we must search the dressing rooms ourselves?'

'Yes,' replied Maurice.

'But we are not used to doing such things . . .'

'Well then we must become used to doing such things.'

'But Maurice, dear,' continued Dennis. 'It has been a very long time since any of us did things.'

Maurice grimaced inwardly - this was true.

'Nevertheless we must locate Octavia's fluffles.'

'But Maurice dear,' insisted Dennis, 'in our world we have others who do things. We would not know how to go about doing things. Surely there are others who can do the thing you are suggesting?'

'Dennis, no. Dennis, no. There is no one else who can do the thing.'

'But there are others who make the tea and clean the floors - why can they not do the thing?'

'Dennis, Dennis, Dennis . . .'

Dennis felt a little awkward. Although he knew that he was speaking for all the members he was uncomfortable about being singled out. He pushed Cuthbert forward a little.

'Dennis,' continued Maurice. 'You know as well as I that others cannot enter the dressing rooms.'

'But surely we can make an exception in this case? This is an exceptional case after all.'

'No exceptions Dennis.'

* * *

It was true. A very long time ago a decree had been decreed which stated that no one was to enter the dressing rooms who was not a Keeper of The Law. No one, for any reason. Whatsoever. No exceptions.

In the C15th someone other than a Keeper had entered the dressing room of a particularly rotund monarch who was in the midst of preparing himself for debate. So startled was the monarch by the invasion that he had jumped almost six inches in the air, causing him to bang his head on something. So grumpy was he by the banging of his head on the something that he let out a fearful roar, and so fearful was the roar that it caused the Keepers to come running into his dressing room and it was in this way that the Keepers spied the monarch's undergarments. And so very deeply embarrassed was the monarch at the public viewing of his hitherto unseen undergarments, which were especially peculiar undergarments, that he went a furious shade of red and the Keepers did not know where to look and they ended up shuffling out of the dressing room and, once outside and quite unable to control themselves a moment longer, collapse in a heap in the corridor and laugh quite loudly. The monarch recovered his dignity, completed his toilette, vacated his dressing room and made his way towards the chamber of debate wherein he sacked the lot of them. Not only sacked but banished them. He would not, he WOULD NOT, have Keepers in his chamber who had been privy to his privy, as t'were.

(Of course without the Keepers of The Law it was very difficult to keep the law and the monarch had to elect a whole new chamber of Keepers which did not make things terribly easy - but that is another story.)

And so it was that the decree had been decreed.

* * *

As no other had been allowed to enter the dressing rooms, no other had cleaned the dressing rooms, and as no other had cleaned the dressing rooms, significantly Octavia's dressing room, a pile of dust and spiders had grown within it and, having been left quite alone due to the lack of cleaning, the pile of dust and spiders had been left to its own devices. And so silent had the dust and spiders been in devising their devices, that as well as being completely unaware of the dust and spiders themselves, which no one had noticed, no one had noticed that the pile of unnoticed dust and spiders had become a mountain - a quite unnoticed mountain.

A small mountain it is true but a mountain nevertheless. And so dusty and spidery was the mountain that not having previously noticed the dusty and spidery mountain, no one could have possibly noticed the addition of extra things which were neither dusty nor spidery, but which were rapidly becoming so. The Keepers peered at the mountain. This was all very confusing.

'What the dickens?' said Maurice.

'Holy mackerel,' said Dennis.

The Keepers shook their heads.

Never in all their born days.

Never in all their born days had they been subjected to such a something. A something which was dusty and spidery and a something which they hoped they would not find similarly in their own dressing rooms.

It really was too bad. Something should be done. Others needed to sort this dusty and spidery mountain out.

'My dear, my friend, my one true love,' uttered Octavia, diving head first into the dusty spidery mountain.

'Eh?' said Maurice.

Octavia stood up flourishing his fluffles. Jubilant and dusty and spidery, but what did he care?

In fact, what did anyone care?

Order had been restored.

Octavia shook his fluffles, sending dust and spiders everywhere, donned it and beamed.

'Gentlemen, shall we?' and with that he led the Keepers out from his dressing room, along the corridor and into the chamber.

'Article 9248,' he said.

'The unpredictably acquisitive behaviour of Dust and Spiders.'

The lady laughed out loud.

Wherein we catch up with Colin Dragon, the Elf's
Guardian Angel, allbehe still a trainee.

Damn and Blast

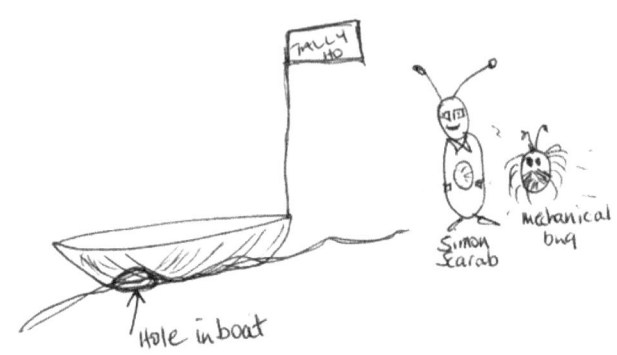

Damn and blast
  Damn and blast
    Damnandblastdamnandblastdamnandblastdamnand
blastdamnandblast
  Damn
  And Blast
  Damn and Blast
  Damn and Blast
  Damn
  And
  Blast
    The Probation Board had caught Colin Dragon out.
They had received news about his foray into the Elf's world
dressed as a washer person.
  Damn and double Blast.

They had re-wired him, him directly, bypassing Simon Scarab and the mechanical bug, so that information about his over flapping would go directly to them. The information travelled by way of a series of minute wires inserted under his left wing which transmitted a rare type of radio wave directly to the Board's monitor in Outer Wherever.

But Colin Dragon was clever.

He was clever and cunning.

He hadn't got to where he was today by taking things lying down. No Siree. He had survived his years in the military and withstood the storming of Mordor along with the other dragons. He had a plan.

He always had a plan.

Colin Dragon had thought about this new situation for a while. And he was bored by it. He thought a bit more and worked out that he could glide from his platform to the seas below with no flapping required. He also worked out that if he attached a long strong rope to a platform leg he would be able to climb back up, again with no flapping required. He very much liked a plan and was happy with this one.

Escape plan decided upon, he foraged around his exceptionally well organised shed. His shed contained stuff which he had kept over the years, not because he thought the stuff would come in useful one day, but because he knew it would.

Long strong rope located he decided to give it a go. Under cover of darkness and balaclava clad he used a double slip and slide knot, wound the rope around the uppermost part of a platform leg, dropped it seaward and then simply stepped off the edge.

Wonderful.

Wonderful to 'fly' again.

The gliding was so graceful that it stirred neither the sleeping Simon Scarab nor the mechanical bug. So graceful was the gliding that the new wire under his left wing twitched not a bit so no message was sent to the Board. He risked a simple double backward flip - again nothing and no one stirred. Aaah, the beauty of 'flight'. The sheer joy of being off the platform cheered him to his very soul (yes, dragons do have souls). And then to hang motionless in the air and enjoy the view around him . . . he rolled over and lay on his back on the wind . . . he whistled a little song to himself . . . and then he continued his graceful glide down to the water.

Plop.

Once in the water he looked around. Nothing to be seen. Inhaling a massive breath he dived. Through the water and down he swam. Again no flapping. He was an excellent diver - in fact he had been one of the last dragons to be used for diving during the battle of the South Atlantic Seas.

On the seabed he spied what he had hoped to spy. A boat. An old boat. An old rowing boat. Using his swishing tail he flippered himself over to it and hooked it onto his back, then gently pushed off up to the sea surface. With no flapping.

It was still dark, but Colin Dragon's eyes were not only bewitching (as we know) but were tuned into the darkness. He had excellent night vision which had saved his bacon, or scales, on many occasions. He dragged the old fishing boat over to a shallower stretch of water and climbed into it. There was a hole in the bottom which he plugged with one of his feet, and then using his tail as a rudder he sailed out across the vastness. 'Tally Ho,' he breathed to himself. He only sailed a short distance, aware that the sun was nudging its way over the horizon and that the fisherfolk would soon be up to claim the waters as their own.

He sailed around the base of his platform and, confident that his plan was a good one, secured the old fishing boat to a leg.

Great. He could do this again.

Slowly he started to climb the exceedingly long climb back up the rope to his platform. Upon arriving at the top he lay down, heart pounding slightly yet still no flaps employed and neither scarab nor bug disturbed.

He fell into a deep and dreamless sleep.

The slightly later morning found Colin Dragon going about his normal business.

Normal and yet so not normal.

The plan he had hatched fired in his belly.

Simon Scarab awoke and read the readings.

'Morning Colin, nothing to report. Nothing untoward then? Lovely.'

The mechanical bug switched and swatched on. Nothing untoward then.

Colin Dragon was impatient to try it again and yet, in deference to the various bugs which and who were bugging him, he went about his day as normal.

'To what has my life been reduced?' he asked himself as he clipped his samphire hedge here and did a little tidying of his mud sculptures forged from memory there. More pottering around he did but later, when the deep darkness descended, he decided to risk it again. He carefully slid down the rope from the platform to the sea below. He untethered the boat.

He was ready for some fun.

And some undercover work.

Purpose. What was to be his purpose apart from the sheer joy of freedom? He decided to see if he could sail a little further out this time.

Unfurling his magnificent wings, and with one foot plugging the hole in the bottom of the boat, he sailed out towards the lighthouse on a distant headland. His great wingspan picked up the wind and he hurtled along, changing direction with the merest twitch. This was great fun. He got a little carried away and started careering from left to right, twitching his wings and feeling marvellous.

'That damned Board,' he thought to himself. 'I can fool them, oh yes, if they only knew, if they only knew . . .'

Bouncing and rocketing over the waves he felt like a young Australian surfer - full of energy and in perfect control of the mammoth sea and his destiny.

Until.

The wind suddenly changed direction forcing him towards the rocks. He needed to alter his tilt but with one of his feet plugging the hole in the boat and his inability to employ any flapping he was unable to do so and could do nothing to stop himself from crashing on the rocks.

He was beached.

Damn and Blast.

Damn and Blast.

Foiled.

Damn.

He struggled out of the boat. Nothing was broken but the boat had suffered a dent in its nose.

'Gotta get back. Can't fly. What to do?'

Damn.

He chided himself for having too much fun, but what was done was done. He felt Simon Scarab stirring under his left wing - yet the wires carrying any sort of detail to the Board remained silent and still.

What to do.

Damn.

Once again the sun was just beginning to think about showing itself. How to get back? And then . . .

A door opened in the lighthouse and the Lighthouse Keeper came out.

'A dragon. Magnificent. Good nearly morning Sir,' he said.

'Um, good nearly morning to you too Sir.'

'How very splendid to see you. One of the military dragons I imagine. Seen much action?'

And strange though it was, Colin Dragon and the Lighthouse Keeper sat down and had a long chat. Turned out the Lighthouse Keeper had also served in the battle of the South Atlantic Seas in the Eager Eagle Force.

'Marvellous days,' said the Lighthouse Keeper.

'Marvellous days,' agreed Colin Dragon.

Fused and forged in the harmony of shared memories, Colin Dragon took the Lighthouse Keeper into his confidence and told him all about the Board. He spoke of the bugs, mechanical and otherwise, which sent messages to the Board who had already clipped his wings and who were very close to stripping him of his current job as Trainee Guardian Angel to an Elf.

'We can't have that,' said the Lighthouse Keeper. 'We didn't get where we are today by being stripped of titles. Let's have a look at the old boat.'

The Lighthouse Keeper surveyed the damage and hurried to the Lighthouse and returned with an old boot. An old boot for the old boat, that'll do it.

Next, the Lighthouse Keeper pulled out his tool bag and together he and Colin Dragon patched up the nose of the boat.

'That'll hold. That'll get you safely back to your platform.'

'Fantastic,' said Colin Dragon. 'Thanks so much. I'd better get on but,' he added, 'I do need to get off that platform from time to time. Mind if I pop over to see you again?'

'My very dear chap,' replied the Lighthouse Keeper. 'Any time, any time. Be a pleasure to see you. And I know how you feel - going round in circles in the lighthouse drives me mad sometimes.'

They shook claws and the Lighthouse Keeper helped Colin Dragon drag the boat away from the shore.

'A word of advice young Dragon,' he said. 'Try to be a little more patient in your dalliances. Try to play the game and the Board will soon become bored with you and release you back to your job. They are recruiting more Guardian Angels - you can't get the staff you know.'

'Good advice. I will do my best. It's just. . .'

'I know I know. But slowly slowly catchee monkey, if you get my drift.'

Colin Dragon smiled. 'I do.'

'Right then. Cheerio Sir,' said the Lighthouse Keeper.

'Cheerio Sir,' replied Colin Dragon, and he swished off into and across the waves until he reached the leg of his platform.

Old boat secured he climbed up the rope, stepped back onto the platform and sat down.

'Good to meet a chum from the old days,' he thought to himself as he picked a couple of herrings out from under his wing.

'Seems a shame to waste them,' he said to himself. 'Breakfast anyone?'

Simon Scarab crawled out into the daylight.

'Don't mind if I do. Nothing untoward? Lovely.'

Lovely.

A Night in the Nights Of

When it's sleep time and the darkness comes (not darkness as in Darkness, three headed monsters, screeching souls, skeletal horses and everyone moaning, but darkness as in the sun has gone down and it's time to sleep) you have to be very careful about what you do with your thoughts. In order to settle down and risk actually getting some sleep you have to let the thoughts out of your brain and into the room. If you are lucky, the thoughts will settle down in a quiet corner, diminish slightly and wait for the morrow. Then everyone is snoring. Success. If you are not lucky, they (the thoughts) will career around the room, bouncing off wardrobes, dressing tables and your bed and get bigger, more electrifyingly interesting, and insistent. At that point you have to call upon the others in your mind who can deal with this stuff with their butterfly nets and yellow plastic fly swats, as you clearly can't - you are too busy watching the ricocheting thoughts and ideas and applauding them.

Or you will have to find a different system.

The following tale is one different system which the Elf thought might work.

* * *

Nice warm cosy tired. The Elf went to bed.

Wash teeth bed.

Book relax book lights off cuddle down.

Relax

Ding

Ignore

Relax

Breathe

Relax

Ding

Ignore

Ignore

Breathe

Breathe

Ding

Ding

Ignore

Ding ding ding

What?

Ding ding ding ding ding

Lights on

Breathe

Breathe

Sit up

Sip tea, calm thoughts (Ding. Ignore)

Calm thoughts. Breathe.

Lights off.
Breathe
Breathe
Breathe
Ding
Ignore
Ding
Ignore
Ignore
Ding ding dingaling a ding donggg!
Sit up
In dark
Close eyes
Put thoughts in black bag
Put thoughts in black bag
See thoughts in black bag
Ignore ding
Take your time
See thoughts in black bag
See thoughts in black bag
Breathe
Ignore ding
Thoughts in black bag
Thoughts in black bag
Ding in black bag
More dings in black bag
All dings in black bag
Tie up black bag
Put black bag in corner of mind
Breathe

Relax

Lie down

Breathe

Breathe

Breathe

Calm

Calm

Breathe

Black bag is moving

Ignore

Breathe

Breathe

Black bag is moving

Ignore

Ignore

Breathe

Black bag is moving

Black bag is moving

Black bag is moving

DING A LING A DING A LING CAN'T GET RID OF US DONGGGGGG

HELP

DAMN DAMN DAMN DAMN DAMN

BREATHE

DAMN DAMN DAMN

HELP

HELP

HELP

HELP

HELP

THAT'S IT
Sit up
Lights on
Tea gone
Lights off
Don't lie down
Don't lie down
And then
And then
And then

The thoughts start jiggling and jostling in the bag, like so many babies in a mum's tum, an elbow jabbing, a knee poking.   Jiggle   jiggle   jostle   jostle   until ******KERPAMMMM****** *the bag bursts open and out shower all the uncontrollable thoughts and ideas and plans and hopes, all together in one almighty swooshhhh as if a massive firework had been lit and sent off to Mars.*

There's no stopping them now . . .

The Elf resigns herself to a long night . . .

This was not going to be easy to control.

The frenzy continues, the thoughts and ideas and plans and hopes fly around the room, crashing into each other becoming muddled and intertwined, coaguled and confused.

The Elf has no need to look after or save the thoughts and ideas and plans and hopes as they are hers and are duplicated in her mind, but she did need some sleep, so she armed herself with a tennis racquet (metaphorically speaking) and set about swatting those she could reach.

15 : 0 – She deals with Money
15 : All – Money fights back
30 : 15 – She slams it into touch
40 : 15 – She jumps on it
GAME

Some of the niggling thoughts were wriggling and oozing along the carpet like caterpillars, they were easy to squish. Others hung from the lampshades and flew off just as she took aim . . .

The Elf imagines another bag, this time stronger than the last and reinforced with thick bands like the seaweed belts around the spring rolls she had had for lunch. She gathers up the squished ones and hurls them into the bag - she uses a cunning backhand scoop with some of the more tricky ideas and then one final overhead smash sees off the What Ifs.

There is now very little movement in the bag but nevertheless the Elf takes the precaution of sealing it tightly with the seaweedy belts, shoves it into a corner of her mind and sits on it.

Squeak

Eh?

Squeak

What?

Let me innnnnnnnnnn

Looking around the Elf notices a very small thought which had been left behind. It was barely worth bothering with as it was just the 'is there any milk for tea' thought, nevertheless she scoops it into the bag with the rest of them.

*(Sometimes, the Elf remembers, it is the weeniest of thoughts
which disturb the most.)*

    Silence
    Still
    Still
    Bed
    Breathe
    Breathe
    Breathe
    Sleep
    Sleep
    S l e e e e e e p
    And tomorrow
    is another night.

Aaaaarrrggghhhh.

Sometimes, thought the lady, we just need to sit down, give in, and breathe.

The Little Hall
A Moment of Peace

The Town Square was busy, but never too busy. Everyone always found a seat. Mrs Johnson took the orders and nobody had to wait for very long.

Folk came to the square to lose their minds, willingly.

Whilst they were in the square, the part of their mind which dealt with worry and pain and unhappiness and bills and unpleasant neighbours and health concerns and domestic issues and all and every manner of troubles, ceased to exist. It was not that that part of the mind left the brain - rather that it shut down as if it had been placed in an hermetically sealed bag and hidden at the back of a dark cupboard at the other end of the house, or in the attic.

Whilst in the square folk sometimes chatted to those around them, but more often they did not. Were they to have a chat it would mostly revolve around charming matters as they had nothing untoward in their minds to which to refer.

Should they elect not to chat they smiled bemusedly and savoured their tea and crumpets, passing the time in a haze of happiness until Mrs Johnson rang the bell. Instinctively the folk left the square and returned to their homes, whereupon that part of their mind which had been inactive burst back into existence.

'Gerald. I have asked you fourteen times to move your bloody bike.'

'Damn you Gillian. I know you are seeing Clithero. Do not deny it.'

'What the hell am I going to do if they make me redundant?'

'Father really isn't well . . .'

'What if I can't get to the hairdresser on Tuesday?'

'Nigel is divorcing me.'

'WILL THERE BE ENOUGH FOOD . . .?'

And so on and so on and so on. And the world continued to turn and folk carried on dealing with their fears and pressures and difficulties but sometimes, in the quiet of a moonlit evening, they would feel the comfort of a moment of tranquillity which nourished their souls and gave them the strength and courage to keep going.

And all because they had allowed themselves to lose their minds.

Mrs Johnson is always available and keeps the tea and crumpet supplies topped up.

Ding-a-ling.

Colin Dragon meets his Match

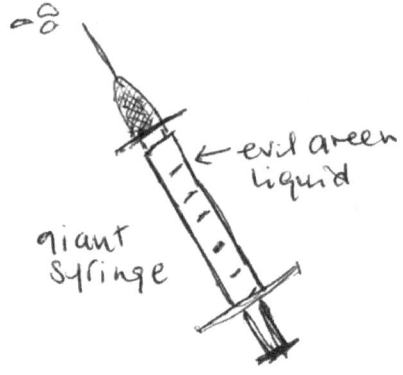

Damn damn and triple damn.

And blast.

Blast.

Blast.

This time not only had Colin Dragon been caught out, but he had been captured. Captured and told off. And sentenced to a spell inside. Bugger.

It would appear that during his latest foray into the world beyond his platform, when he had to fool both the bug who was bugging him and the bug who had been sent to monitor the bugging bug, something not quite right had happened to the wires which connected him to the Probation Board for them to monitor his behaviour. And this something which had happened had caused a short circuit between the wires and the monitor. The wires which had been inserted under his left wing. His wing. His wings were the very heart of him. The very heart. Of him. His heart. His heart.

So he had been caught out by the Probation board, captured, told off and summoned to answer for his misdoings.

* * *

The dragon was on the couch. Strange image, yet true. No-one was doing very much talking. Colin knew that it would be useless to resist. He knew that too much trouble from him would result in being shackled by the white coats. And the one thing that Colin hated more than being monitored, was being bound. By anything really. But mostly by rules and shackles. So the mighty dragon lay belly up on the couch, attached to a large machine by a series of wires.

'Now Colin,' said the 'doctor'. 'Relax. This will not hurt,' and his eye glinted, momentarily, as he whipped out a large syringe from the drawer in his trolley of implements.

'Lie back,' said the 'doctor', 'and Colin, please, do relax. We want to help you. Now,' he continued as he strolled around the couch, his hands behind his back, 'it is important that you remain perfectly still Colin. This need not take long and it need not be painful - unless of course your mind touches on things that are painful to you. We need to understand more about your 'condition'. We plan to question you and it is of paramount importance that we know the truth.'

Colin raised an eyebrow.

'The truth Colin. You have been rather selective in that department in the past, if not to say downright meddlesome. In fact so cataclysmically untrustworthy in the whole truth department have you proven yourself, that it has been decided that in order for us to discover more about your

condition I am going to have to drug you.' He did a little knee bend pirouette. 'And it is you who has forced this particular outcome, Colin. You have brought this upon yourself.'

The white coat circled the couch and returned to his trolley of implements. He picked up the excruciatingly large syringe and jabbed it into a phial containing a curious green liquid.

'This drug will make you think of strange and odd things,' said the white coat as he drove the entire phial of green liquid into Colin's wing. Colin looked around him. 'Yes, and when will you administer the drug?'

'I have already done it,' smiled the whitecoat, and with another steely little glint he prepared and administered a second dose.

Colin floated up to the ceiling and using his index claw pulled a chicken from his left ear.

The whitecoat left the room.

'I am the Dragon who walks alone . . . or am I a cat . . .' he said as he started to fall under the spell of the drug . . . 'the cat who walks alone?' . . . and then he started to talk about this and about that and about all and everything he had done . . .

(Colin was not really on the ceiling and he did not have a chicken in his ear. It was a mighty powerful drug.)

The door to the consulting room swung open and Miss Doings sashayed in. She had the casual air of a French secretary about her. Tortoiseshell glasses, plaid suit, hair swept into a chignon with a jaunty flyaway piece over one eye.

Colin was still rambling . . .

Miss Doings sauntered over to the couch and sat down on the chair that had been placed next to it. She took out her notebook.

Colin rambled on about battles and jousting and underwater missions and rocket powered fast cars and circling the moon and whipping up storms and roundabouts.

'Is there anything you haven't done?' interrupted Miss Doings.

'Yes,' said Colin, suddenly dragged back from the psychedelic tunnel of his reverie by the silkiness in Miss Doings' voice.

'And what might that be?' asked Miss Doings.

'I have never worn a cardigan.'

Miss Doings made a note of this.

Colin and Miss Doings continued to chat.

'Can I call you Yvonne?' asked Colin through his haze.

'If you wish, yet my name is Mina,' replied Miss Doings.

'That's a strange name,' said Colin.

'As strange as Colin?' said Miss Doings. 'Tell me, Colin. Why do you flaunt authority so? You could have a very nice life but you will insist on pushing things.'

'Yvonne look,' said Colin, swishing an oversized metal beetle from the wall to his right. 'I have fought the most dreaded creatures in Mordor,' swish 'I have stood tail to fin with some of the bravest dragons in the Universe. I have pitted my wits against the underwater monsters and the snarling cacklebirds, and now . . .'

'Yes Colin? And now?'

'And now I do the ironing.'

Miss Doings smiled. 'Well, that is not all you do nowadays Colin.'

The drug was beginning to wear off and Colin strained to rise above the couch.

'That is not all you do nowadays Colin.' repeated Miss Doings.

'True, but a Trainee Guardian Angel . . .'

'Which position carries a certain gravitas . . .'

'To an Elf,' interrupted Colin.

'And had you not continually transgressed the rules of your position you would have graduated beyond Trainee by now.'

'To an Elf. And an Elf who doesn't require much guardianing these days.'

Miss Doings continued her questioning as Colin slowly regained his brain. He had learned a great deal during his time in the fighting corps. He had especially learned a great deal about questions. About how to ask questions and especially how to ask a question without anybody knowing they were being asked a question. And about how to avoid being asked questions, how to not answer a question or indeed how to answer a question without the questioner knowing he was, or wasn't, answering it. Or, in fact, how to avoid letting a questioner know that he was answering a question even if he weren't. Confusing stuff.

Miss Mina Doings knew a thing or two too, and they spent a very pleasant couple of hours each double crossing the other. It was something like a game of mental chess.

Colin and Miss Doings were getting on so well that Colin burst out 'Yvonne. Come on. Let's get out of here.'

'I'm with you Colin,' came the joyous rejoinder.

'Great. Okay, a plan. What have you in your make up bag?'

Miss Doings dug her make up bag out and opened it.

'Eye shadow. We need all the eye shadow we can get,' said Colin.

'Surely you are too large and green and scaly to disguise yourself with a little azure hue?'

'No no Yvonne. We will create a distraction. Come on now, all of it.'

Miss Doings took the various eye shadow palettes from her make up bag and put them on the couch next to Colin.

'Right. Next a light bulb.'

Miss Doings unscrewed a bulb from the ceiling light. And carefully, carefully, Colin removed the tiny filament from the glass bulb and carefully, carefully, tipped the powder eye shadow into the bulb until it was filled with the grey green blue powder. (Amazing how dexterous a dragon's talons are.) He then replaced the thread connector and handed the bulb back to Miss Doings.

'If you would,' he said.

Miss Doings screwed the bulb back into the ceiling light.

'Right,' said Colin. We know what to do. You are sure Yvonne?'

'I am Colin.'

Miss Doings opened the door of the consultation room.

'Help,' she cried. 'Help help,' throwing in an 'Au secours,' for good measure.

Footsteps were heard coming down the corridor.

Colin winked.

The door flew open and then BAMMMMMM!!! As the whoevers entered the room, Miss Doings threw the light switch and there was an almighty PFFFFFFFTTTTTTT as the grey green blue exploded into the room and they all thought they had been shot.

Colin and Miss Doings belted from the room, and although Colin had been schooled to fight not flight, he knew when he was licked - besides he was rather good at flying. Colin knew that he had a possible five seconds until the mist cleared in the room, so he signalled to Miss Doings to climb aboard and out they scarpered and, on crashing through the third floor window they did indeed take flight . . . and a very beautiful soaring sight it was.

Colin flapped for all his might.

Damn that Probation Board - he would work out a plan when they were safely back on the platform.

Try to outwit a Colin Dragon? 'You can't kid a kidder,' he smiled to himself.

Positivity is all very well and good . . . but sometimes it can drive you bonkers. But I will try to stay solid and take my joy where I find it, the lady said to herself, with a slight grimace.

The Little Bedroom
Pollyanna

Pollyanna bounced along the street. It seemed that everyone needed her at the moment.

* * *

Pollyanna hadn't realised that she was different until she was about nine. And not different in a wandering around with two heads way, just different.

She had found that as she went through her day nice things would happen. She thought that nice things happened to everyone, but it seemed that wasn't necessarily so.

For example.

At the corner of the street near to her little school was a sweet shop. Pollyanna had a sweet tooth and she would often pop into the shop on her way home and gaze in delight at the tall jars filled with multi-coloured sweets. One day when she popped in for some humbugs Mrs Brown was in quite a state. Mrs Brown was huffing and blowing and was red in the face.

'Is there something wrong?' asked Pollyanna.

'Very wrong. A new delivery man came with my order this morning and everything is all jumbled up. The mints are mixed up with the bonbons and as for the acid drops, well.'

'Let me help you,' said Pollyanna. 'I am sure if we try to untangle the jumble together everything will soon be back in order.'

Mrs Brown and Pollyanna started re-organising the jumble, quietly and methodically. It didn't take long before the sweets were in the right jars. Apart from the acid drops, which had spent so long next to the jellybeans that one had flavoured the other.

'Have to chuck them out,' said Mrs Brown. 'No good to anyone - jellybeans tasting of acid drops simply won't do.'

'Unless,' said Pollyanna, 'unless you can market them as jellybean variable?'

'Might work,' smiled Mrs Brown. 'No harm in trying. Now then, what can I get you?'

'I'll take a quarter of jellybean variable please and thank you.'

'You shall have them on the house,' said Mrs Brown, measuring the new variety of sweet into a twisted cornet of pink and white striped paper.

'Thank you Mrs Brown,' said Pollyanna as she took the sweets.

'No no, thank you,' said Mrs Brown.

Pollyanna left the sweet shop. Mrs Brown sat down. 'Just as well Pollyanna came along,' she thought to herself as she popped a jellybean variable into her mouth for a taste test.

'Hmm. Strange but yum.'

* * *

Pollyanna went to see her Grandpa. She loved her Grandpa. He was not in a good mood however.

'What is wrong?' she asked him.

'Pesky rats,' he said. 'If I were to sit here long enough I would see 'em. Little snouts peering at me from the flower bed indeed.'

'What do you mean,' Pollyanna asked.

'Each night when I sit out here with me pipe I hear 'em scratching and scritching. Drives me mad.'

'But have you actually seen them?' she asked.

'No, my eyesight is dimpsy and my hips ain't what they used to be so I can't get down to their level, but if I could, I would do 'em in . . .'

'Grandpa. I will sit with you and we shall see,' said Pollyanna.

They sat together in the cool of the evening and heard the scratching and the scritching. Grandpa said 'Bah, can't be bothered, my bed is calling.'

'What can I do. Shall I wait?'

'You could have a dibble around in the soil and tell me what you see,' said Grandpa.

Duly, Pollyanna took up the trowel and dibbled around in the soil.

'Nothing here,' she said.

'That'll be because they have gone, you will have scared them off with your dibbling,' said Grandpa.

'Or maybe,' said Pollyanna, 'maybe the noise you hear is simply next door's cotoneaster scratching against your fence? Maybe there are no rats?'

Grandpa went inside.

Pollyanna sat quietly and after a little while saw a very small rodent creature. She smiled.

She went in to find her Grandpa.

'Grandpa, it is just a little fieldmouse scratching and scritching around in the soil.'

Grandpa frowned and he thought, and then he smiled.

Pollyanna smiled.

All was well.

(At some point during this story you may have hoped that Pollyanna would have shouted Bugger or Damn and Blast. But she wouldn't. It simply isn't her way.)

And we all know people who are genuinely lovely. And positive. And optimistic. But sometimes you just want to grab them by the throat and say 'LOOK, damn you. Yes, yes, I know all that positive stuff. But please, please, leave me alone. Just let me be miserable and furious and fed up about it for tonight!'

The Elf and the Most Marvellous Musical Major had become firm friends through the buying and selling of houses and the sharing of their experiences when dealing with the humans and other creatures who offered the houses for sale. The Estate Agents. The Most Marvellous Musical Major was becoming increasingly discontented with the world in which he worked. And in many ways yearned for an alternative existence . . .

The House of Pain

THE HOUSE OF PAIN

The Most Marvellous Musical Major had donned his armour. He had inherited some items from both of his beloved grandfathers. He wore the breastplate from his maternal and the gauntlets from his paternal. He carried his cricket bat and his special pen. He was going into war. Not a war when he would have to kill someone, but a war nevertheless.

The Most Marvellous Musical Major worked in the Land of Law.

He was terribly good at his job.

He was honest and true and swift and pleasant and (mostly) always did what he said he would do when he said he would do it. The Most Marvellous Musical Major helped folk to buy and sell houses.

That bit was okay.

He found out things about their houses and made sure that they were safe and steady.

That bit was okay.

But this day was different. This was a Friday. And each and every Friday was the same.

* * *

Many years ago, when humans wanted to buy and sell their houses they would make an agreement, the buyer with the seller, and they would spit on their hands and then shake each other's hands and all was well. Then they would call in a Legal Human who would write things down so that there could never be any doubt that the buyer had sold to the seller and that they had agreed.

This system carried on for many hundreds of years, from the days when humans inhabited caves until the days that they moved from the countryside and entered the towns. But not very long ago in the history of the humans something had shifted.

A certain group of creatures began to smell an opportunity.

An opportunity they had spied and smelt where they could elbow their way into the hitherto customarily gentle experience of the buying and selling of houses. At first only a *few of these creatures became involved - muscling in between the buyer and the seller.*

They would take one of the parties aside and whisper in their ears.

They would whisper things such as: 'Do not trust that fellow . . . He has a glinty expression.' Or 'I can get you more money - leave it with me guv'nor.'

And words such as these hypnotised the hitherto happily uncomplicated humans and made them greedy and they turned to these creatures and instructed them to get in the middle between they, the seller/buyer and the others, the buyer/seller.

Time passed.

The word spread amongst the creatures that some of their fellow Rats had started to earn serious money and receive presents from the humans for whom they were 'working'. More Legal Humans were needed as gradually the Rats began to take over. Soon it was impossible to walk along an ordinary street in any part of Old Englandshire without bumping into these Rats. They all, without exception, wore shiny suits and they all, without exception, smelt bad. (As they had previously been living in the sewers they had a certain smell about them that passed from generation to generation. When they started to inhabit the houses akin to the houses they 'helped' the humans to buy and sell however, their particular smell had become mixed with cheap red wine, garlic and dolcelatte. A heady and most unpleasant concoction.)

Soon many of the local shops disappeared as the Rats opened more and more 'agencies'. These were places where the Rats could inveigle humans in, sit them down on their plush multi-coloured seats, offer them a bottle of overpriced water and then, with the help of some soft soap and a flannel, seduce the humans into letting them 'help' with the buying and selling of their houses.

Now, the trouble with something that seems to be too good to be true is that it usually is. Gradually and by degrees (180° to be precise) the humans began to realise that they were being taken for a ride - and a bumpy one at that. The Rats, or Agents as they liked to be called, did not always do what they said they would do on the day upon which they said that they would do it, and they were not honest and true.

In fact they lied.

They lied quite a lot and they bullied the humans.

So on this particular Friday when the Most Marvellous Musical Major went into his work in the Land of Law (he called his office The House of Pain) he knew what (or rather who) he had to face.

The Rats.

* * *

Friday was the day upon which the Rats received their money if all the papers concerning the houses that they were 'helping' the humans to buy and sell had been ticked and signed. The Rats did not care about whether the buyer or seller were happy, they simply wanted their money and with salivating dribbly leering greed they lined up in front of the offices of the Land of Law and started shouting.

In the House of Pain the Most Marvellous Musical Major steeled himself.

'Don't panic Sir,' he said as he stepped outside. (He often talked to himself in the third person and in a military fashion as it helped him focus and gave him courage.)

On spying the Most Marvellous Musical Major the Rats pushed and shoved each other, all eager for news of their sales.

''Ave you finished number twenty-nine?' one Rat called.

'No,' replied the Most Marvellous Musical Major.

'Eh? Why not?' the Rat shouted back.

'Hold up with the Bank,' replied the Most Marvellous Musical Major.

'Wot about Hillview Cottage?' shouted another Rat, 'All done wiv?'

'No,' replied the Most Marvellous Musical Major. 'Too much damp, buyer withdrew.'

'OH WOT?' the Rat yelled before stumbling off, kicking at the dust. He knew he would have no money that day.

'And me,' screeched another Rat. 'What about me? How about 47 Wibbly Way?'

This went on and on. The Most Marvellous Musical Major was very patient. He was also very clever. He had worked out a long time ago that he only needed to use $1/10^{th}$ of his Marvellous mind when answering the Rats' questions and, being Musical, he found it helpful to play beautiful music through the other $9/10^{th}$ of his splendid mind so he was (mostly) able to listen to the chords of a song rather than the desperate gnashings of the Rats. His chosen song on this particular Friday was The Great Gig in The Sky and he hummed the chords (under his breath of course) and found a little solace. (He had been playing this particular piece of music the previous evening on his piano at home and had thought that it had sounded rather good - but then he remembered that he had had one too many glasses of Old Butter Porter, so perhaps it hadn't been.)

The questions went on and on.

Some of the Rats were jubilant as their deals had gone through and they left dancing and prancing and showing off as they caroused up the street towards the nearest house of ill repute. (They had clubbed together and 'bought' this house - or stolen it, some humans had said - as no one else would have them and they needed somewhere to shout and show off and spend their ill gotten gains.) Others shook their heads and left, empty handed and disgruntled. Someone was going to get a kicking. Some of the even nastier Rats bared their teeth at the Most Marvellous Musical Major and, coming right up close to him, pushed their hairy sweaty faces into his and breathed cruel threats and warnings at him through their stinky yellow teeth.

It was for these incidences that the Most Marvellous Musical Major carried his cricket bat. With a few deft strikes he shot the hideous creatures into outer field calling 'Six' as they landed wherever they landed.

Very slowly the long line of Rats disbanded and all was done.

'Excuse me?'

The Most Marvellous Musical Major started up the steps to return to his office to continue with his work.

'erm, hello?'

It was going to be a long day, there was still so much to do.

'Please Sir?'

The Most Marvellous Musical Major thought he had heard a tiny something, and on looking down spotted an extremely small fieldmouse.

'Yes, can I help you?' he said.

'I hope so,' replied the extremely small fieldmouse. 'It has long been my dream to help humans and other creatures with the buying and selling of their houses.'

'Okay,' replied the Most Marvellous Musical Major frowning a little. 'But you know that the job is being done, albeit badly, by your colleagues the Rats?'

'Yes, I know that. I know they do a simply dreadful job and I want to change all that. And we may all be rodents but we are most certainly not colleagues.'

'Fair point,' said the Most Marvellous Musical Major. 'But you are extremely small and they are mean and many. How do you think you are going to muscle in on their business?'

The Most Marvellous Musical Major and the extremely small fieldmouse sat down on the steps of the offices and started talking.

The extremely small fieldmouse reminded the Most Marvellous Musical Major about the Land of Dreams and what one has to do to make a dream come true. Together they hatched up a plan of how the extremely small fieldmouse could infiltrate the Rats' business. It wasn't going to be very difficult really as the extremely small fieldmouse would be honest and true, and it wouldn't take long for the humans to realise that there was someone 'proper' with whom they could work.

The Most Marvellous Musical Major and the extremely small fieldmouse shook hands (the Most Marvellous Musical Major being careful not to fling the extremely small fieldmouse into touch) and said goodbye.

'By the way,' said the extremely small fieldmouse, 'what is your dream? Everyone has one you know.'

'Ah,' replied the Most Marvellous Musical Major, 'I should like to travel to the Land of the Pink Flamingos, or maybe the Land of Plentiful Herbs, and find some other fellows and play my music on the beach.'

'What a beautiful dream,' said the extremely small fieldmouse. 'And when shall you realise your dream?'

'Oh,' said the Most Marvellous Musical Major, 'when I have changed my car and finished sorting out my filing and found the right moment and . . .'

'Hmm,' interrupted the extremely small fieldmouse. 'Do not leave it too long. I have known humans and other creatures leave their dreams for so long that they forget that they had had the dreams in the first place.'

The Most Marvellous Musical Major frowned again. 'Well, I do intend my dream to happen.'

'Intention is good, but action stations, my dear new friend, are better. Stand by your beds and keep alert. Make your dream come true and I will sell you a very fine house in the Land of Plentiful Herbs. (For the Land of the Pink Flamingos is frankly too pink.)'

They shook hands again and the extremely small fieldmouse left.

The Most Marvellous Musical Major turned and went back into The House of Pain. He looked at his filing cabinet.

'Phooey,' he said to himself. 'Enough for one day.'

On returning home the Most Marvellous Musical Major opened the lid of his piano and played as he had never played before. He played a wonderful song with a sting in its tail.

He played Moon over Bourbon Street. Then he sat down and had some.

Then he smiled.

The Most Marvellous Musical Major had opened the lid of his mind and the dream was growing.

Confusion Abounds
The Study
'Stay clear of Armley,'

he had said.

She wondered why.

* * *

Jeremy chucked the waistcoat into the laundry basket.

Damn that smoke.

He kicked off the shoelets, unpoppered his poppered trousers and finally took a breath.

Damn.

* * *

Back at the club they were talking. How could he have been such a fool?

'Yes, but did you see the size of them?'

* * *

Humans and other creatures thought Jeremy strange.

True he was rather tall even for a reptile (over eight and a half feet in his socks).

True he wandered around in spats (when most of the more sensible world were wearing Clarks).

True he had an attitude.

But that wasn't it.

None of these traits made Jeremy strange.

The strange thing was that he could sing. But not in the usual way for a lizard (or anyone) to sing in the late 80's, with rock, new wave and post-punk abounding. No. Jeremy did Sinatra. Jeremy was a crooner. His voice was as smooth and silky as a hamster skin rug.

And because he could sing, and because humans and other creatures liked his style, and because he had a certain way with him he was always booked. Sometimes he wondered whether they came to see him because he was different, but he didn't mind. He liked to sing. He loved to sing. When he sang it was as if he were all alone in the world - floating around on his personal cloud of loveliness. And he was happy. Very happy. BUT.

He did not like people making fun of him. So what if other singers were wearing sparkly jeans and tee shirts, or worse still those shiny tracksuits in neon colours? So what if the men had floppy hair and looked like girls? Jeremy had his own style. And he was happy with it. Jeremy loved the films and stories of life in another time. A time he believed to have been more gentle and calm than now. A time when romance was elegant. Elegance. Elegance. His favourite word. So Jeremy dressed in spats and pin striped trousers and a shirt and tie. Sometimes a bow tie. Sometimes a cravat. But always a tie.

* * *

Jeremy stepped out of the shower and slipped on his satin dressing gown. He felt better. He crossed to the sitting room and hesitated momentarily in front of the drinks trolley. 'Gin sling or Martini?' he pondered. Martini. He poured just the right amount of vermouth and vodka into his favourite deco glass, popped in the olives and crossed to the terrace with a little twirl. Then he sat down, picked a Havana from the silver box and took a sip from his glass. Delicious. He lit the cigar and took a long pull. Delicious. Not like those filthy fags they smoke in the club he grimaced.

Could life get any better? The ugliness of earlier seemed almost a distant memory and with very little extra effort Jeremy was able to put it out of his mind. Completely out of his mind. He leaned back in his chair. His favourite chair. He observed the Armley skyline (not overly attractive but it was what he had) and hummed the opening bars of 'My Funny Valentine' to himself. Bliss. Complete and utter bliss.

In many ways Jeremy was happy in Armley. His hunger for the bright lights of Leeds had ebbed with the passing of time and he was happy with what he had grown to love. Sometimes he felt like a big fish in a small pond (or similar simile) and he was happy with that. There was, after all, no other lizard threatening his position at the top. The top of his particular game that is. He had friends and enough money to pay his bills and keep the cupboards stocked. He even had enough to pay for the sushi he had sent over from Japan every now and again.

'Yes,' he mused to himself. 'Things are pretty good around here . . .'

BANG.

BANG.

BANG.

'What the . . .?'

BANG.

BANG.

BANG.

Someone was hammering on the door.

BANG.

BANG.

BANG.

Jeremy grimaced. There were some pretty unruly people in his block.

He put down his drink and cigar and walked towards the door.

BANGGGGG . . .

'Yes, yes,' said Jeremy. 'Who is it?'

'Derek,' said Derek. 'It's Derek. DEREK. D E R E K.'

Jeremy grimaced inwardly. Damn.

'Derek. Go away. It's late. We have been through all of this. I have nothing more to say.'

'You have nothing more to say?' yelled Derek. 'You have nothing more to say? Well I've got plenty more to say Jeremy. PLENTY.'

Jeremy, aware that Derek was intent on staying there shouting until he opened the door, opened the door. He could not stand scenes. What would the neighbours say?

Derek folded in his antennae so that he could get through the door.

'Right. Right. Right then. Right then Jeremy. Right then,' he taunted.

Jeremy sighed. He had been through all of this. Why did this bloody oversized earwig insist on badgering him?

'Drink Derek?'

'Eh?'

'Drink Derek?'

'Oh . . . Uh . . . Don't mind if I do . . .'

'What'll it be?'

'Eh?'

'What'll it be Derek?'

'What are you having?'

'Vodka martini Derek.'

'Same as you then,' said Derek ('smooth bastard' under his breath).

'Olive Derek?'

'Eh?'

'Olive Derek?'

'Uh, thanks.'

Jeremy prepared the martini and popped in the olives. He signalled to the terrace. 'Shall we?'

They went out and sat down. Jeremy re-lit his Havana and took a long pull.

'Now Derek. This has got to stop. We have been through this. We have been through this, all of it, before. You are going to have to drop it.'

Derek took an ugly slug of his martini. Elegance was not his favourite word.

'Damn you Jeremy. I can't drop it. I love her.'

'Yes, yes. I know that. You know that. And so does Melissa.'

'I can't drop it. I can't drop it. The way she looks at you . . .'

'Derek. She is looking at me because I am singing. I am singing on stage and folk look at me. They look at me because I am singing.'

'Yes yes, but the way she looks at you . . . the way she looks at you . . .'

'Derek. Melissa loves you. You know that.'

'And then . . . that song. You had to sing that song. You had to sing that bloody song. That bloody song. That bloody . . .'

'It was on my request list tonight Derek.'

'But that song . . . that bloody song . . . that bloody song . . .'

'And what is so wrong with that song Derek?' Jeremy asked, gliding towards the drinks trolley to prepare two more martinis.

'You know damn well. You know damn well. You know damn well.'

'What? What?' asked Jeremy humming a little of the song under his breath.

'Well . . . it's, you know . . .'

'What?'

'Well . . . you know . . . suggestive . . .'

'Suggestive?'

'Yeah - you know, suggestive . . .'

'Suggestive?'

'Yeah - you know, you know . . .'

'I fail to see how that song is more suggestive than any other Derek.'

'You know . . . you know . . .'

'No, I don't know.'

'Yes, yes you do . . .'

Lizard and earwig took a deep sip of their martinis.

'Hmmm,' said Jeremy wisely. 'I think I may understand where you are coming from Derek.'

'You do? You do?'

'Yes. But he doesn't mean it literally.'

'Eh?'

'He doesn't mean it literally - not literally under his skin.'

'Aaaarrrgggg . . . you see? You see . . .'

'No Derek I do not see. And neither does he literally mean "deep in the heart of me."'

'Aaaaarrrgggggggghhhhh . . .'

'Nor "so deep in my heart that you're nearly a part of me."'

'Aaaarrrgggggggghhhhh . . .'

'It's not literal Derek. It is not literal. He does not mean it literally.'

'Well. Well. Well then . . . well . . . what does he mean then?'

'It's poetic Derek'

'Eh?'

'It's poetic. He means that he loves her so much that he feels they are entwined forever in the close tenderness of their love.'

'Aaaarrrgggggghhhh . . .'

'Their love Derek. *Their* love. It is a love song Derek. I sing love songs. I sing many love songs. It is what I do. I sing love songs. What on earth is your problem?'

'Melissa. The way she looks at you . . .'

'Yes we have been through that.'

'No . . . the way she looks at you when you sing that . . . that . . . that bit . . .'

'Which bit?'

'The under your skin bit aarrrrggggghhh . . .'

'Derek,' (Oh God, under his breath). 'Derek. It isn't literal.'

'Yes but you . . . you are a lizard . . .'

'Yes yes?'

'And you shed your skin . . .'

'Yes?'

'Therefore if somehow you managed to get Melissa under your skin . . .'

'(Oh God) yes?'

'Well. Well then. Well then. You'd just bin her.'

'Eh?'

'If you were to get Melissa under your skin, at some stage you would bin her.'

'(God) what on earth are you blithering on about?'

'You . . . you skin shedder. You'd inveigle her under your skin only to shed her, with it, at some later stage . . .'

'Derek. Derek. Derek. Another drink?'

'Yes damn you.'

Jeremy went to make the drinks. He realised he was going to have to deal with this situation rather delicately. It is true that he sheds his skin, but always discreetly. And elegantly. But how on earth was he going to get Derek away from his misunderstanding of the meaning of the song and his misconception of Jeremy's feelings towards Melissa and the possible likelihood of him shedding her at some stage, with his skin, were he to get her under it in the first place, which he wouldn't. Aaaaarrrrrrgggggghhhhh.

He returned with the drinks.

Derek was looking twitchy. More twitchy than is usual for an earwig and his now extended antennae waved curiously in the early morning breeze.

Jeremy knew he was going to have to outwit a nitwit of an earwig. And quickly. Derek was getting drunk.

'Derek. Is that why you sent the boys?'

'Hmm?'

'Is that why you sent the boys round tonight?'

'Dunno what you mean,' swig.

'The boys. To the club. Tonight.'

'Errrr . . .'

'The boys, to the club, tonight, looking for trouble.'

'Errrr . . .'

'Yes Derek. Errrr indeed.'

'Hmmmmmm . . .'

'Derek. Look. I forgive you for that, but I will not, not, have my performances disturbed by a couple of oversized earwigs with a grudge. Gettit? Comprennez? Capiche?'

'I, umm, I didn't know what else to do . . .' sip 'the way she looks at you . . .'

'Yes yes - we have been through that. But why send the boys? You know a couple of mothy earwigs are no contest for my tail?'

(It was true. When Dave and Bill had stormed the stage - if stormed is the right word for a pair of overweight string vested insects clearly looking for trouble - Jeremy had rippled the muscles in his tail and with one broad swipe had sent them flying into the wings. Everyone had cheered except the bouncers who were concerned that their jobs may now be at risk on evenings when Jeremy was performing if the bosses of the club got to hear of his bravery. They made a point, later, of telling all and anyone who was interested - and there were not many - that Jeremy was a fool. 'Should stick to singing and leave the manly stuff to us' they said. No one cared.)

Jeremy took a deep breath.

'Right Derek. Concentrate. Let me try to explain something to you. Listen carefully. I shall say this only once. Firstly, as discussed, Melissa loves you. Secondly, Melissa looks at me because I am singing. Not because she loves me. In fact, historically, earwigs are rarely attracted to lizards largely because most lizards are not vegetarian. Thirdly, given that Melissa loves you and is not attracted to me, it is unlikely that she would allow herself to be inveigled by me to get under my skin. And fourthly, and perhaps most importantly, if, IF, IF I succeeded in inveigling Melissa under my skin, which will not, not, happen, remember that I am able not only to shed my skin, but to shed it in sections should I wish. So even if Melissa were actually and physically under my skin, I could deposit her safely in an agreed place at any time. There.'

Jeremy wiped his brow. This really was all too much.

Derek was thinking.

'You mean. . .?'

'Yes yes yes Derek. Yes.'

'You could pop her somewhere safe?'

'Yes.'

'She would not be lost to me?'

'No.' (God help me.)

'Right.'

'Right?'

'Yes. Right Jeremy. I get it. I see.'

'You see?'

'Yes. Cheers.'

Derek got up to leave.

'So we are okay?'

'Hmm?'

'You and me. We are okay now?'

'Yes. Sure. Cheers Jeremy. I didn't know that bit.'

Give me strength. 'So you understand facts 1 - 3?'

'Eh? Yes sure. But the last bit . . . You can't win Jeremy. You can't win. So back off my babe.'

Jeremy put his head in his foot.

It had been a long night.

'Cheers then Jeremy. See you around,' and so saying Derek got up, folded in his antennae and left the flat.

Jeremy blinked at the dawning Armley skyline.

'Maybe I'd fare better in Leeds after all . . .'

Interlude
The Bicycle of Sleeplessness
A shortish conversation

'I seem to be trapped in a cycle,' the Elf had said to Little
Lily that morning. *'A bicycle of sleeplessness.'*

*And there we have it. The Elf started a conversation
with herself which went like this:*

'Well then, if it is a bicycle you can always get off.'

*'Not possible,' she told herself. 'It seems to have a life
of its own.'*

*'But that is not possible,' she argued. 'And you are
either on it or not.'*

*'It is not that simple. I don't think I got on the bicycle
on purpose, yet on it I am, irrefutably.'*

'Well stop pedalling then.'

'Can't.'

'Why not?'

'Because if I take my feet off the pedals they go around by themselves and I continue to career through the dark bit.'

'The night you mean.'

'Yes, the night.'

'Tried putting the brakes on?'

'No good, rusty.'

'You or the brakes?'

'Both.'

'Hmm. So what are you going to do? You need to get off that bicycle.'

'I know that - but how?'

'Take control and change direction?'

'Done that but am still on it - in whichever direction I hurtle.'

'Tried taking a picnic?'

'Eh?'

'A picnic. You could pack a picnic and pop it in the bicycle basket and then you could stop for a rest.'

'I like it. I will give it a try, yet I will still have to get back on.'

'Have to?'

'Yes.'

'Why so?'

'Because it seems the bicycle is in control and not me and no matter how much I lie about on the grass I shall still have to get home again.'

'Eh?'

'Well otherwise I will be stranded in a perpetual dejeuner sur l'herbe and that will be as bad as being stuck on a bicycle.'

127

'You need to get out more.'

'Maybe so.'

'How about a contra-visualisation?'

'What the fiddle?'

'Well if as you say you are stuck on a bicycle when you should be slumbering peacefully during the dark bit, try seeing yourself somewhere else.'

'Yet still on the bicycle?'

'Well yes, if you are unable to leave it.'

'Maybe a penny farthing?'

'Sorry?'

'Maybe I could swap bicycles and get on a penny farthing.'

'Why?'

'Because they are large and cumbersome so even if I am still on a bicycle I could ride more peacefully through the dark bit. It might be more soporific?'

'It could work.'

'Worth a try?'

'Why not.'

'Or how about this, why not park up in one of the mayor's bicycle rests.'

'But then you would still have to get off and that, you say, is the problem.'

'Hmm.'

This exchange went on for some time, yet the Elf had to pop to the market for some weekend fare. She knew she would be thinking all the time though which would make it hard to select a bean.

Beans selected.

'Market trolleys are a bit like bicycles,' the Elf said to herself, 'and they really do have a life of their own as they go off in a completely different direction from the one which you are intending. Going forwards in brain, turned left by dint of trolley. And the wheels get stuck.'

'Perhaps, but you were able to leave the trolley.'

'Well of course. What do you think I am? Some kind of complete weirdo who is unable to leave her market trolley behind?'

'No it's just that if you are able to do that . . .'

'No no no no no. You really don't get it do you? It is not that I am unable to leave things with wheels behind in true life and during the daytime, it is just not the same during the dark bit.'

'Hmm, you really are odd. Now listen, I have had an idea.'

'Yes?'

'How about you plan an accident?'

'An accident?'

'Yes.'

'As in?'

'Okay. You fall off the bicycle.'

'But that is the same as getting off.'

'No it isn't. You fall off the bicycle and then you pretend to be unconscious.'

'I fall off the bicycle and pretend to be unconscious?'

'Yes.'

'In the dark bit?'

'Yes.'

'So I wait for a while until I think the bicycle isn't, what, listening or paying attention and then I fall off it?'

'Yes.'

'I don't know which is weirder.   That you are suggesting I try to fool an inanimate object which doesn't actually exist, or that I am having this conversation with you.'

'Well that's nice.'

* * *

A little later . . .

'I have it!'

'What?'

'Eureka!'

'What?'

'The solution!'

'Alright with your exclaiming and marks and all . . . tell me.'

'You must BREAK THE CYCLE.   Ta daaah.'

'Break the cycle?'

'Yes, break the cycle.   It's the only way.'

'You mean smash up the bike?'

'Yes, basically.'

'But if I can't get off it how am I do break it?'

'Do it in the light bit.'

'Eh?'

'In the day time.   When you are not trying to be asleep.'

'So during the day time I smash up a non existent bicycle?'

'Well it's either that or endless hours of Midsomer Murders.'

'Help me Lord. Why?'

'To numb your brain.'

'But we are my brain.'

'Yes, I know that, but maybe you, or rather we, have to numb ourselves before we try to go to sleep.'

'Sleep by boredom?'

'Maybe . . .'

This too-ing and fro-ing went on for too long a time until the brains decided to try everything. Picnics, rusty brakes, fooling the bicycle that they were unconscious, the smashing up of a non existent bicycle and also sleep by boredom.

But not Midsomer.

Maybe the whole of a re-run of Downton. That could do it.

And you wonder why we don't sleep?

Exactly.

The lady often had too many emotions which she wore all at the same time on her sleeve, which wasn't always a good thing.

The Spare Bedroom

Once upon a time in the Land of Hidden Tears

Moira pottered off towards the well. The buckets were particularly heavy this morning.

Daniel wrung out his handkerchiefs and hung them out to dry.

Brenda mopped the kitchen floor.

* * *

Long ago, the King had decreed that it was forbidden for his subjects to show their feelings.

He had decided that emotions were a sign of weakness. He feared his enemies would take advantage of any emotional outpouring and attack his realm in the squidgy soft bit. And he could not cope with the thought of that.

He would not, NOT be overthrown.

So every morning or week or month or whenever the tear water threatened to overspill the containers, the people would go to the well, or the river, and empty them out.

It was the same with laughter. The King had decided that any loud and joyful noise would also interest his enemies. Hearing any chuckling or guffawing - by an individual or, heaven forfend, by a group - would surely suggest to his enemies that his subjects had lost their minds and therefore be easy to defeat.

The people found it as hard to conceal their laughter as their tears and made a point of only sharing jokes or quips when behind closed doors. If any of them felt the uncontrollable need to laugh out loud whilst in public, they were forced to stuff tissues or handkerchiefs into their mouths so as not to release the slightest titter.

And then there was love. Public displays of love were entirely unacceptable. So upon greeting a long lost friend, or welcoming a new baby into the world or finding a cat who had been lost, they had to remain entirely impassive.

These rules forced the people to extend their houses so that they had more space in which to gather together and express themselves. Emotions, as we all know, are extremely powerful and cannot be entirely supressed. So the people shared their love or pain or joy whenever they could, or whenever they needed to, and they had developed a peculiar form of sign language to enable them to communicate the need as and when it arose.

There was also to be no shouting or swearing or spitting in the street. If people wanted to fight there was an underground room where they could punch each other. Mind you by the time they had descended the 4270 steps, they had invariably got over their gall and pretty much forgotten what the gripe had been about. Brian had set up a bar down there and instead of fighting they usually had a beer and told a few jokes.

* * *

You may find it strange, but interestingly the people did not revolt. However repressed they may or may not have felt, they respected their King. These rules of his had been in place for a very long time and they had become used to them. (Of course the second generation had known no other way of being.)

In so many ways their King was fair. He rarely increased the taxes. He provided excellent housing for people with little money and ensured that a doctor was always available should they need one. He set up a council who genuinely listened to the requests of the people and tried to help whenever possible. And he supported the Arts (which was interesting as some would say that creativity in any form is the way that emotions are displayed and explored and shared). It was often hypothesised (over a couple of beers) that the King believed that for the people to display their emotions through their Art removed the need for them to make a fuss publicly.

* * *

Early one morning a figure entered the square. Wendy. The sister of the rival King.

She approached one of the guards, said something to him and was lead to the Palace.

'I crave permission to live in your lands,' she asked the King. 'My brother does not feel things the way you and I do. He does not support the Arts. Why, he makes it so difficult for any of us to actually create anything that by the time we have filled out his many forms, in triplicate, we have become numbed to the beauty we wished to paint or write about.

The King furrowed his brow.

'But if you come here to live your brother is sure to storm my castle and take you home.'

'No no. On the contrary. I have become too troublesome to him. I am a Warrior for all the

Artists in his lands. He is planning to banish me. He will be delighted if I move out and live here.'

And so Wendy lived peacefully in the land and created some of the most amazing Art the world had ever seen. But that is a story for another time.

* * *

So how were things to change?

You might have thought that when the King's Mother died his rules may have been relaxed, such was the reported outpouring of his grief (in private, of course). But this did not happen.

You might have thought that the raining gold coins, which randomly occurred one morning, may have inspired the King to relax his rules. But this did not happen.

You might have thought that when his Royal Football Team won the cup the King may have relaxed his rules, such was the (supressed) joy he felt. But this did not happen.

You might have thought that when the real rain rained over the land and a hitherto dead Royal Forest was reborn the King may have relaxed his rules. But this did not happen.

You may even have thought that the growing friendship between the King and Wendy may have inspired him to relax his rules, so twinkly were his eyes on visiting her studio and so enamoured had he become with both her and her Art. But not even this changed the King's mind. He did not relax his rules.

The people carried on, resigned to the emotional aridity of their existences.

Until one day . . .

* * *

One quiet calm Spring morning, the dew lying undisturbed in great globlets and all was well and fresh with the world, and the birds were singing and the fields were shimmering lush with the newly planted crops and (you get the picture?) . . .

One quiet calm Spring morning a hazy figure appeared on the horizon. Slowly, slowly the figure advanced towards the town. Slowly, slowly the people saw that it was a man. A man, thin and pale.

As he passed by the people gasped (gasping not having been banned).

The man's beard was long and ragged. His hair was long and ragged. His fingernails were long and ragged. His robes were long and ragged. But his eyes. His eyes twinkled in a way the people recognised. The word went round. It went around and about the town and ended up in the Palace.

The King appeared at the top of the Palace steps. The man was at the bottom. He leant against the wall but now unable to stand, stumbled and collapsed.

'My Boy.'

The King descended the steps two at a time.

He reached the crumpled man at the bottom and let out a yowl. The yowl shot across and around the square and into the sky.

The King bent down and picked up the withered man.

He cradled him in his arms, took a deep breath, and sobbed.

He sobbed long and loud and uncontrollably.

Slowly the King carried the shrunken figure up the steps and in through the Palace doors, which closed silently behind them.

The Guards were not sure what to do.

The people were not sure what to do.

They cranked themselves back into their day and carried on as usual, aware that something strange and big had happened.

* * *

A week later smoke was seen billowing from the Palace's enormous chimneys, soon to be followed by the most marvellous aroma.

Guards passed amongst the people telling them that there was to be a feast in the Palace grounds that evening, and that they were all invited.

'And wear something bright and jolly,' they were told.

'Bright and jolly?' they said to each other, brows furrowed.

At the appointed hour (which is always six o'clock no matter where you live in the world) the people filed through the gates which led into the Palace garden. And what a sight did they behold.

Tables were piled high with food of every delicacy they could imagine (and some they couldn't), jesters were jingling around the place and a band of minstrels were playing happy music.

'Eat eat,' called a voice and looking up they saw the King descending the steps.

'Eat my friends, eat,' he called, and the people helped themselves to the feast and began to eat.

But then a trumpet sounded.

'Ba ba ba ba ba ba baaaaaaaaaa.'

A handsome figure walked down the steps. A figure (slightly on the thin side it is true) who passed amongst them, smiling, and who went to sit next to the King who asked his people:

'Do you remember him? Most of you will. Twelve years. Twelve years since I lost him. Since he disappeared that night. But now he is back. My son has returned to me'.

The people clapped and cheered and the King beamed.

'My friends,' he continued with tears in his eyes' (yes, tears) 'I have to tell you something rather strange,' he chuckled (yes, chuckled). 'My son did not leave for the love of a good woman, nor was he dragged kicking and screaming from his bed by some foul beast or, heaven forfend, by my enemies. No. He left because of greed. His greed, his own greed,' (more tears) 'he thought he would fare better elsewhere. He thought he could make an easier and greater fortune in the lands beyond . . .' the people gasped and shuffled their feet - they were not sure what to expect.

'But,' continued the King. 'But. He has seen that he was wrong and foolish. He has understood that to rule can be a blessing as much as the curse he once thought it. He has realised that his destiny is to be here, amongst us, and that one day he will take up the mantel and lead you all. And,' the King added, fanning his face and quite overwhelmed by the emotions he was feeling, 'and he has begged my forgiveness.' The King had to sit down. But he had not finished speaking.

'My Son. My Beloved Son. You do not need my forgiveness. A parent's love is unconditional as you will hopefully discover yourself one day. But you may need to speak kindly with our subjects. I imposed a pretty arid way of life when you went away and it has been hard for them - they may not forgive you so easily.'

The Prince stood up and opened his arms to the people, tears streaming down his face.

'I am sorry . . . I am . . .' was all he could manage.

Silence.

And then . . . the people whooped and hoorayed and clapped and cheered, tears streaming down their faces . . . they hugged each other and went a little bit mad.

The King signalled the minstrels to play some dancing music. He nodded at his son to open the celebrations.

The Prince turned to someone standing not very far away from him.

'Shall we?' he asked Wendy.

Decisions Decisions . . .

Or

Dark Happenings in a Really Nice Place

The Most Marvellous Musical Major wandered the streets of Silentios. He had returned to the Land of Plentiful Herbs for one last look before he made the final decision - Herbs or Flamingos.

The Most Marvellous Musical Major was considering leaving Old London Town and retiring to a place where there were no rats nor annoying humans or other creatures and spend his days improving his jazz piano skills. He thought he might even form a small jazz group and play beautiful music on the shores of the deep blue sea and be happy, always and forever.

The Land of Plentiful Herbs was indeed beautiful and interesting and peaceful. But did anything ever happen here? Sometimes it seemed a little like Midsomer, a small inconsequential village buried deep in the Englandshire countryside which was, he imagined, a nice enough place but where nothing ever happened.

The other land to which he was considering retiring was the Land of the Pink Flamingos. He had also visited that land on numerous occasions and although, as most of his friends would say, it is rather too pink, it is vibrant and exciting and a person knows that a person is alive when in the Land of the Pink Flamingos.

Pottering down the little cobbled alleyways en route for his morning coffee, the Most Marvellous Musical Major admired the architecture and the colours and the quaint and creaky heavy oversized doors of the little houses. And the herbs. Always the herbs. Planted in any sort of container the folk could find. Parsley and sage and basil and chillies and oregano and coriander and all and every kind of herb and each and every one. The Most Marvellous Musical Major picked his way amongst the fragrant herbery down the steps which led to the town square.

'Hola,' said the Most Marvellous Musical Major to the air around him.

The square was deserted.

The Most Marvellous Musical Major seated himself at one of the little iron tables and waited patiently. It was very quiet and he wondered if he had made a mistake and that it was in fact Sunday. Eventually however Dromederios, the café owner, brought him his coffee. He noticed that Dromederios was limping rather badly.

'Bonjour Dromederios, you seem a little stiff today, back playing up?'

'Morning Most Marvellous Musical Major, no, ankle,' replied Dromederios.

'Hmm. Had an ankle once. Bloody painful. Gout they said. Or rather pseudo-gout. All very odd.'

Dromederios frowned. His English was pretty good but words such as pseudo-gout befuddled him. Those words befuddled most people unless you were a rheumatoid specialist and then you would understand very well. Bloody painful.

'No bells today?' asked the Most Marvellous Musical Major.

'No, no bells today, κύριος.'

Dromederios seemed to have the hump. He placed the cup on the table and hobbled back to the café.

The MMMM (let's for the most part call him that – we all know who he is) took a gentle sip of his coffee and dipped the little cake into the froth. Delicious. He looked around and smiled. 'It really is pretty here,' he thought. 'But so quiet. I wonder if I could stand it . . .'

He took another sip of coffee froth and dippy cake and wiped his mouth on his napkin. 'Hmmm, yes . . . I wonder,' he wondered.

Caught in a reverie of silence and following a train of thought that led him to wonder whether he would go stark staring mad in the silence, he at first failed to notice a whirring sound. He picked up his cup again. 'Delicious coffee.' He drained the cup.

He pulled himself into the here and now and then . . . then he heard running. He heard loud and heavy running. Footsteps were advancing down the narrow street, and after an agonisingly tantalising moment a whirling dervish of small leaves burst into the square.

Tomas.

Tomas hurtled around the almost deserted place. He seemed not to notice the MMMM. He hurtled around, zooming in and out of the four corners of the square. He ran hither and thither. He ran hither and thither again. This was a very strange way for Tomas to behave.

Tomas was a Thyme Traveller. He travelled the length and breadth of the Land of Plentiful Herbs gathering and selling thyme. Hence his job title. And he was used to travelling hither and thither but not all in one go and not all in one small square.

'No no! Help help!' he shouted as he whirled around.
'No no! Help, help!
No no! Help, help!
No no! Help, help!
No no! Help, help!'
(What he actually shouted was:
'Όχι όχι! βοήθεια, βοήθεια!
Οχι όχι! βοήθεια βοήθεια!
Οχι όχι! βοήθεια, βοήθεια!
Οχι όχι! βοήθεια, βοήθεια!
Οχι όχι! βοήθεια βοήθεια!'
but for the purpose of re-telling this tale we will stick to the english. Besides which it was all greek to the MMMM.)

Tomas continued his frantic whirling.

'Calm down man,' said the MMMM - who had the ability to calm even the most whirlingy of humans and other creatures. Tomas came to an abrupt halt next to the *MMMM*'s table.

'Sit down and tell me what has happened to make you behave so. Dromederios,' he called 'another coffee for me and something for Tomas.'

The Most Marvellous Musical Major decided that Tomas needed a beer, and when Dromederios appeared with more coffee he ordered a στιγματισμένος παλιά κότα for him. This could have been confusing but Dromederios was used to the *MMMM*'s greek and so instead of bringing an actual old speckled hen, he brought a beer. The *MMMM* thought this particular beer would go nicely with the thyme. Ever thoughtful.

Tomas took a long slug of the beer. He took another. He took another long slug and a glug. Delicious. He appeared to be calming down slightly and most of him had stopped whirling. Apart from some of the smaller leaves.

'So, what is going on?' asked the *MMMM*.

'It is terrible, terrible. Terrible things are happening. Terrible terrible terrible things,' Tomas spluttered, draining his glass.

'What terrible things?' asked the *MMMM*.

Tomas lifted his head from the glass.

'There has been a run on Rosemary,' he groaned, visibly shaken.

'Eh?'

'Yes.'

'What?'

'Yes.'

'Not?'

146

'Yes.'

'Eh, what, not . . . Not whatnot?' gasped the MMMM as the information slowly began to sink in.

'Yes,' said the distraught Tomas. 'It is true.'

The MMMM called out for Dromederios to bring more beer and decided to have one himself. This was no time for coffee.

'Not a word to Dromederios mind,' said Tomas. 'If this were to get out . . . '

'Quite,' said the MMMM.

Dromederios brought the beers and was happier now that he had customers to serve. It wasn't always this busy.

'So. Tell me all about it. How did you find this out?' asked the MMMM.

'I have been looking for Rosemary all over the town. I have been everywhere. We were due to meet on the steps of the church today at midday. But she is gone. Οχι οχι, βοήθεια βοήθεια, οχι οχι, βοήθεια βοήθεια, οχι οχι, βοήθεια βοήθεια . . . '

'My dear Tomas,' interrupted the MMMM. 'Try to control yourself, although I must agree this is indeed a calamitous happening.'

The MMMM considered becoming hysterical but managed to pull himself together. One of them had to remain stable.

'But, Most Marvellous Musical Major, Rosemary has gone and all the rosemary has gone. We go so well together. We were made for each other. I really thought we had a future.'

Tomas downed the last drop of beer and threw his head upon the table and began to shake it furiously. A rain of thyme leaves flurried around the square.

The MMMM realised that this was an extremely tricky situation. Back in Englandshire he was used to dealing with matters of a legal nature, but this was completely different. Here and now, in the Land of Plentiful Herbs, not only was he required to deal with matters of the heart but also attempt to avert a potential culinary crisis. This was going to require tact, guile and a certain genius.

He ordered more beer.

The two men sipped their beer. Tomas was mostly still, although his forehead did a lot of furrowing and frowning. The MMMM searched his mind for words of comfort.

'I am sure Rosemary will turn up Tomas,' and then 'did you have a tiff by any chance?'

'A tiff, Most Marvellous Musical Major?'

'Yes, words . . .'

'Words?'

'Yes, words. Did you have an argument?'

'No no Most Marvellous Musical Major. We never argue. We are happy together . . . we were made . . .'

Tomas' eyes became creaky and crinkly. They filled up with water and the MMMM was afraid that the quasi stability of the situation would be lost if Tomas continued.

'Right. Okay. Umm . . . Well now . . .'

Both men took a long pull on their beer.

(The MMMM, being terribly British, did not always find it easy to speak of matters of the heart. This was perhaps *why he immersed himself in his piano music, allowing the melancholic chords to say more than he ever could. Tomas on the other hand, being of a latin bent, was fair overflowing with emotional utterings.)*

'Rosemary, Rosemary. How I love her. How I love Rosemary. My Rosemary. Without you I shall perish. Οχι οχι οχι οχι οχι οχι οχι . . .'

'Come Man, we must be positive.'

'But she is my love. She is the one. The One . . .'

The MMMM put a consolatory hand on Tomas' shoulder.

'My dear friend, if I may call you that, we shall make a plan, we shall . . .'

The MMMM was truncated in mid sentence by something curious. A strange smell pervaded the air. He looked at Tomas. Tomas looked back at him. He continued looking at Tomas and then . . . Mentos strutted into the square. (The MMMM always thought that the smell of mint resembles cat pee. On this occasion he kept his thoughts to himself.) Mentos strutted into the square in a way that implied he thinks he is god. Not God you understand, but a god.

'You . . . you . . . you . . .' spluttered Tomas, pushing back his chair and leaping to his feet.

'Yes it is I,' replied Mentos.

'Your visit to this place at this time can mean only one thing.' said Tomas.

Mentos folded his arms.

'You have stolen my Rosemary. You have stolen my Rosemary and you have stolen the rosemary.'

'Shhh,' said the MMMM. 'Caution, even the walls have ears.'

'You do not deny it?' said Tomas.

Mentos stood, arms folded and feet wide apart. His lip curled in an unattractive sneer. Tomas saw red. Tomas stepped back. He grabbed a stalk of thyme from his head and hurled it to the ground.

'You want to fight me?' breathed Mentos.

'I will fight you. I will fight you for Rosemary and for the rosemary. I will fight you for honour and for the woman I love. Besides which we are nowhere without rosemary.'

Mentos twirled around the square. Sure he was bigger than Tomas, yet his heart was empty. Not only that but he had the most basic of culinary skills.

There was going to be a duel. Herb on herb.

The two matadors (as they now viewed themselves) paraded around.

The MMMM was nervous.

Dromederios, who had come out of the café to see what the fragrance was all about, was nervous.

Were there a band available they would have played March of the Titans. There was no handy band however.

'If there is to be a battle I shall be your second,' said the MMMM bravely, and stood in the far corner of the square next to Tomas.

'No no dear Most Marvellous Musical Major. 'This is my battle. I shall fight alone.'

Our beloved MMMM, quizzical now as to the outcome yet sure as eggs is eggs (as they say) that no good would or could come of fighting, sat back at his table.

'Rosemary and Mentos, it is not a common combination,' taunted Tomas.

'Yet we have worked well together in the past,' replied Mentos.

'That maybe so but it is just not classical,' retorted Tomas.

('One – zero,' thought the MMMM.)

Tomas took a swipe at Mentos.

Mentos retaliated with a body blow.

Then the two herbmen tumbled around the square, locked in a vicious brawl of arms and legs and twigs and leaves.

Tomas was bruised - the smell of thyme filled the air. ('Such a delicate aroma,' thought the MMMM.)

Mentos was cut. He released the acrid smell of cat pee and the MMMM shuddered. ('Good for Pimms though,' he thought to himself. 'Bit of cucumber and a few strawberries. There's a place for everything in this world . . .')

The fracas continued. Leaves flying all around and about the place. This was getting nasty. Tomas' fragrant aroma was being overridden by the more pungent one.

Dromederios had an idea. He hobbled as quickly as he could towards the church crying 'The bells, the bells . . .'

Unseen by the flailing duo, Dromederios, having found the door locked, started to clamber up the wall of the church. He was determined to ring those bells. He was determined to ring them loud and long. He would stop these ridiculous shenanigans if it killed him. (He hoped that it wouldn't kill him, he had a lamb kofta in the oven. Which lacked rosemary. 'Hmm, and I need some mint for my dip,' he thought as he climbed.)

The duelling duo continued their battle.

The square was strewn with the herby mix.

The MMMM had started chewing a finger nail and was wondering whether he should in fact do something, if only fetch a bowl, when suddenly

'BONGGGG.'

A bell was heard.

'BONGGGG.'

And then 'BONGGGG BONGGGG BONGGGG BONGGGG BONGGGG BONGGGG BONGGGG,' with a little 'cling clang cling,' thrown in.

The dishevelled herbmen stopped.

The MMMM stopped.

The door of the church flew open.

Nothing happened.

The three looked at each other.

'Clingggg, clangggg, bongggg,' said the bells.

Then silence.

As the leaves settled around the square another aroma became noticeable.

Tomas lifted his head, currently under Mentos' foot, and there she was. There was his Love. There were all his hopes and dreams wrapped up in several long twigs.

'Rosemary,' he spluttered. 'Rosemary my Angel of Loveliness.'

Raising his arm Tomas ripped Mentos' foot from his head (which action hurled the darkly cut smelly Mentos half way across the square), leapt to his feet and raced towards the church.

Rosemary was running down the steps.

They fell together at the bottom, infusing each other with their aromas.

'Rosemary and Thyme,' thought the MMMM. 'Can't beat it.'

Mentos limped away. He knew it was all over.

Dromederios slipped back to the café and prepared a large jug of Ouzo.

Rosemary explained to the assembled company that she had gathered all the available rosemary and taken it to the church. She had been decorating the church prior to her midday rendezvous with Tomas. She had hoped very much, she said, that the two would become one.

'You mean . . .?'

'Yes Tomas. I want to be with you for all time. We are a classic combination and together we will make beautiful stews and fish dishes and . . .'

The Thyme Traveller had found his Rosemary. As they embraced the air became heady with a very special perfume.

Dromederios and the MMMM winked at each other, re-filled their glasses, and went in search of several bowls.

'Waste not want not,' the Most Marvellous Musical Major said to Dromederios.

'Indeed my friend, indeed.'

'*By the way, genius to think of the bell ringing . . .*' and the two men pottered about the square collecting the fallen leaves.

Much later that evening the Most Marvellous Musical Major had to smile.

'*Like Midsomer?*' he said to himself. '*Not really. Nothing ever happens there, but here . . .*'

Frustrated by the non-achievement in finding a shop, the lady took a pitch at a local market where she met Derek the Farmer - and they exchanged tales and became firm friends and remain so to this day.

Pigs out til 8

Derek drove the fifty miles back to The Farm. It had been a good day. He had been to a Farmer's Market and he was the Farmer. He smiled as he replayed the goings on at the market in his mind, and thought about the sausages and chips which he always prepared for the other market traders, and how there never seemed to be enough. 'Greedy lot,' he smiled. To Derek the other market traders were his extended family and he liked to feed them. He liked looking after others.

So musing and singing along to Meatloaf he drew nearer to his precious fields.

Passing through the green lush in the early evening light he looked from left to right and back again, performing his nightly check.

All was well.

He pressed on along the winding lanes, tired but happy. Turning the last corner and spotting the smoke furling from the chimney of the farmhouse, he almost missed something.

Almost.

He stopped.

He reversed his beautiful new truck.

What?

Yes.

There.

A gate.

Left open.

A gate.

A little ajar . . .

He pulled up adjacent to the gate ajar and stepped down from the truck, shining the light from his powerful torch into the field.

Everything seemed normal. Yet although everything seemed normal, Derek knew instinctively that something was amiss.

He swept his torch light into and around the far corners of the field.

And then he spied a shape. A lumpy shape with a small glow at one end.

Quietly he passed through the gate ajar, closing it behind him as he entered the field. He turned off his torchlight and stepped towards the lumpy shape with a small glow at one end.

(He was not afraid. These were his fields. He had loved these fields since he was a boy and with every passing year his love for them grew. He felt as if he knew each and every blade of grass and each and every clover stem.)

The lumpy shape grew larger as he drew nearer.

Derek screwed up his eyes.

Madge?

Could it be Madge?

It was Madge. One of his favourite Tamworths. Smoking a cheroot propped up against a straw bale was Madge, looking rather worn out.

'Madge?' said Derek. 'What are you doing here? What's the problem?'

'Ah Derek. There you are. You're late,' replied Madge.

'I am a little late yes, but what's up? You should be tucked up in your sty by now.'

'Couldn't sleep.'

'Couldn't sleep?'

'No,' puff.

'Why Madge?' (Derek feared that Madge might have been sent out to announce some sort of revolution. Derek always feared there might be a revolution. He had, after all, just returned from market where he had gained a handsome price for some of the meat.)

'It's Jim,' said Madge, taking a long drag on her cheroot and wiping her forehead with a trotter.

'Jim?'

'Yes. It's Jim. He is not happy.'

'Not happy?'

'No. Jim is not happy. In fact Jim is not at all happy.'

'Jim is not happy? Why not Madge? I like to think that all my animals live a happy and fulfilling life before . . .'

'Before we reach the end. Yes Derek. And we do. We are all happy and well looked after.'

(Derek heaved an inward sigh of relief.)

'So?'

'The chickens have relocated.'

'Eh? What?'

'The chickens have relocated.'

'And that is why Jim is not happy?'

'Yes.'

'And why does anything the chickens do make Jim unhappy?'

'Personal space.'

'Sorry?'

'Derek, look. We all live together. We live happily and we rub along and we do not fear the end.'

'But?'

'Well it's the principle of the thing really.'

'The principle?'

'Yes Derek. The principle. We rub along and we are happy and we are well fed and looked after and we do not lack anything. But we must have our personal space.'

'But you do . . .'

'We need our personal space Derek. We have thoughts. We have thoughts and dreams and hopes for the future (how ever short our time may be) and we like to snuggle up from time to time with our loved ones and sometimes, sometimes we just like to be.'

'To be?'

'Yes. To be. Silent and tranquil. And alone.'

Derek was a little confused. He had not honestly thought very much about his animals' hopes and dreams. Stupid really, he thought. Not stupid that his animals had hopes and dreams but that he had not considered that they did. Or what they might be. But, he reminded himself, if he honestly knew the depth of his animals' hopes and dreams he may not be able to . . . and then where would he be?

* * *

Madge had finished her cheroot.

'So,' said Derek. 'Personal space?'

'Right. Look Derek. This free range farming ethic of yours is to be applauded. There is not one animal on this farm who doesn't think so. We all respect you.'

'Even though I . . .' interrupted Derek.

'Yes, even though you . . . That is simply the Order of Things Derek. We all know the score. You raise us and we happily live out our lives. In many ways we are pretty well off. There is no subterfuge here Derek. We understand the deal and we accept our fate. You will find no Orwellian gestures here. And, unlike many other animals, we were not born into slavery, none of us is bound or gagged and we have the freedom to roam until the day we don't.'

Derek blushed. 'Yes, and?'

'Right. Apart from all of that you should remember, Derek, who we are. That pigs, as a breed, don't mind inhabiting small spaces. We are never happier than when in a pen not much larger than we are. So, much as we love and appreciate the freedom to wander, we don't mind if we can't.'

'U-m-m.'

'But when we go to our pens or stys Derek, when we return home to our small but perfectly formed residences . . .'

'Y-e-s . . .?'

'We want to be alone.'

'R-i-g-h-t . . .'

'Alone Derek. Alone.'

(Derek struggled to remove the image of Madge in a trench coat from his mind.)

'And Jim?'

'Jim has got chickens.'

'Eh?'

'Derek. It has become cold. How many eggs do you normally collect a week in warmer weather?'

'Hundred or so.'

'And how many eggs did you collect, say a couple of weeks ago?'

'Twenty three.'

'Exactly. And how many eggs did you collect yesterday?'

'Nine.'

'There you have it Derek. And what do you think explains the diminishing egg productivity?'

'The cold . . .'

'Yes Derek. The cold. You know that and I know that. So the chickens have relocated to Jim's sty. You can't move for albumen in there.'

'You mean?'

'Yes Derek. The chickens have relocated and are laying in Jim's sty.'

'Well blow me down. I thought the chickens were not laying because of the cold. . . I had no idea that they were laying elsewhere. I thought they had just stopped for the moment and it's true, I haven't been into Jim's sty for a good few days.'

'So what are you going to do about this situation Derek?'

'Hmm. Could it wait until the morning? I promise I will find a solution only Brenda will have the, um, supper on and I am pretty well done for. Would you tell Jim that I will sort it out?'

Madge lumbered up to leave the corner.

'Derek?'

'Yes, Madge?'

'I trust you.'

Madge waddled off in the direction of her sty.

Derek scritched his head and stood watching her leave, pondering for a while.

When he eventually arrived at the farmhouse his wife was fuming.

'What sort of time do you call this?' she spat. 'It's past eight.'

'Sorry love, had a bit of a problem on the way home.'

He knew Brenda wouldn't understand.

He grimaced as she put his supper on the table.

Pork chop.

Interlude
Oozing from Ankles
(or, As We Age)
for Leila

The Most Marvellous Musical Major's sister was soon to pass a milestone and cross a stile on a particular path. It wasn't a stile too high nor was the path covered in brambles and nettles. It was an ordinary path which cut through the rolling fields and hills of good old Englandshire. The Most Marvellous Musical Major's sister felt okay about crossing the stile, yet her daughter felt otherwise and constantly teased and taunted her mother about the fact. She talked about it to the Most Marvellous Musical Major and his friend, and a conversation ensued.

* * *

'When you get old,' said the Most Marvellous Musical Major's niece, 'you get diseases which ooze out from your ankles.'

'Oh no you don't,' said the Most Marvellous Musical Major's friend.

'And,' continued the Most Marvellous Musical Major's niece, 'you lose your hair.'

'Oh no you don't,' replied the Most Marvellous Musical Major's friend.

'And when you get old,' continued the Most Marvellous Musical Major's niece, 'you start to forget - you forget everything.'

'Oh no you don't,' replied the Most Marvellous Musical Major's friend. 'In fact you remember more.'

'And when you get old, you get grumpy and picky and you smell,' said the Most Marvellous Musical Major's niece.

'Well,' said the Most Marvellous Musical Major's friend, 'none of that is true. When you become older, as all of us will - even you,' she nodded at the niece, 'you become more sensitive, more forgiving, more able to understand very big things and actually you smell better. You smell of life and experience and that has a very particular smell which we shall discuss another time.'

The Most Marvellous Musical Major's niece frowned.

'And,' continued the Most Marvellous Musical Major's friend, 'a while ago I set you a mathematical problem. I asked you how large a pile of mouse poo would be if a person decided they would rather eat their own body weight in mouse poo than do a certain thing. Have you an answer for me?'

'Well, erm, no' replied the Most Marvellous Musical Major's niece. 'I thought that it was a silly question and that you must have been joking.'

'No I wasn't joking,' replied the Most Marvellous Musical Major's friend. 'In fact I have worked out the answer myself. You see when you get older you learn many things. You learn how to think in colour, how to see around corners, through glasses darkly and you learn to recognise the density and direction of a teardrop. So no, I wasn't joking. Come back when you have an answer for me.'

The Most Marvellous Musical Major's niece and the Most Marvellous Musical Major's friend said goodbye and went their separate ways in their very different worlds, the Most Marvellous Musical Major's niece frowning and the Elf smiling a little smile.

How things change as we age, thought the lady. Not always in a bad way, just in a different way . . . and we have to learn to change with them.

And All around grow Old and Frail
The Kitchen
Girl in a Café

Jocelyn sat in the café with her cat. Each had a chair. It wasn't entirely normal for a cat to be on a chair in a café, but Parker was immensely fond of a latte.

Jocelyn stared dreamily out of the window.

The café owners, Ramiro and Ramez (pronounced Rameth) were quite used to the girl with the long hair and her cat popping in for coffee.

They knew exactly what Jocelyn would order and were already bringing it before she did.

'Au lait for you an'a latte for'a Parker,' said Ramiro as he placed the two steaming cups on the table.

'An'a 'ow are things?'

'Thank you Ramez,' said Jocelyn, 'things are just fine.'

'Ramiro,' said Ramiro. (They were twins you see, and it was often difficult to tell them apart.)

'An'a you Parker?' said Ramiro, pushing the latte closer to Parker's nose.

'Oh, he is fine too - everything is fine, everything is rather peachy actually,' replied Jocelyn.

Jocelyn stirred her au lait and continued to dream her dreams. She was quite awake but in another world. She was often to be found in another world, her own little world. And, she had discovered, life was often sweeter in the dreamworld in her head than in reality.

(Many years ago Jocelyn's mother had pointed out that she thought Jocelyn was a dreamer. 'She's a dreamer that one,' she had said, 'lives in a cloud. Like a butterfly. In a cloud of her own, except that a butterfly in a cloud wouldn't be able to see where it was going . . . oh dear oh dear.' Jocelyn's mother was a bit of a dreamer herself.)

Ramiro and Ramez were au fait with Jocelyn's ways and had grown fond of her over the years, so although the café was buzzing around her (and they could sometimes do with her table) they left her to it and smiled. ('She'sa off again, in'a her own little world,' their smiles told each other. Twins don't always have to actually speak to hear what the other has to say.)

Parker took a teeny sip of his latte.

Parker was not feeling himself.

Parker was getting on in years and somehow his taste buds were not tasting the way they should. His brain knew that he loved latte, but his internal organs weren't sure today. He wiped his whiskers with his paw.

Parker was renowned for being rather a dapper cat. Were he human he would most probably enter cafés with a little swagger. Were he human he would probably carry a silver topped cane and he may even sport a trilby worn at a jaunty angle. But he was not human and even though Jocelyn loved him totally and utterly she was so preoccupied with her own thoughts that she did not notice his rather sombre expression. (Cats have expressions too and the one Parker was wearing today was decidedly glum.)

When Jocelyn had come to the end of a particular line of thought in her mind, she picked up her cup and drained the now tepid au lait.

'All done Parker?' she said. 'Let's away then.'

Parker was not all done but he felt all done, if not to say done for and done in. Slowly he oozed his way down the chair leg and waited at the door of the café for Jocelyn to pay the twins.

'Thank you Ramiro,' she said to Ramez. 'Lovely as always. See you tomorrow.'

'Ramez,' said Ramez. 'Goodbye Señorita, 'av'a a wonderful afternoon.'

(When Jocelyn and Parker had vacated the table Ramiro quickly laid it up and served the twelve people who had been patiently waiting. The twins really did like Jocelyn. And Parker. Very much.)

Jocelyn sauntered along the pavement, picking up an avocado and a few plums from the fruit stand near to her apartment. She also bought some white fish for Parker's supper. Parker was extremely fond of white fish. She bought some shiny mackerel for herself and some bright pink flowers.

'What a beautiful afternoon,' she said to Parker. 'An afternoon for flowers and as I am feeling particularly jolly today they must be pink. What do you say Parker?'

Parker managed a squeak. Squeaking was not normal for Parker but Jocelyn didn't notice.

Jocelyn climbed the iron staircase up to her apartment.

Parker took his time.

Jocelyn opened the door and skipped around the apartment, smiling to herself.

Parker hadn't yet made it up the stairs.

Jocelyn was thinking about Bernard (pronounced Bernaaaaard).

Bernard, Bernard, Bernard.

Jocelyn poured herself a glass of wine (pink, of course) and continued with her reveries.

Parker was half way up the staircase.

'Bernard,' she thought. She picked up her glass and went into her bedroom

'Maybe one day . . . maybe one day I will be brave enough to talk to him.'

Parker had just about made it to the top step.

Jocelyn brushed her hair and then remembered Parker. She went out onto the balcony and called him. He had just arrived on the little iron platform.

'There you are Parker,' she said. 'Come on,' and she scooped him up in her arms and twirled with him into the kitchen.

As Jocelyn prepared Parker's fish she continued to think.

Jocelyn was not entirely sure what she wanted to 'do' about Bernard. If 'do' was the right word. Jocelyn was not entirely sure if Bernard thought anything about her. She was not entirely sure whether Bernard realised that there might be something to 'do' about him. It was all rather confusing.

Jocelyn put Parker's plate down and pottered into the sitting room. She sat down, leaving Parker to snack in the kitchen and thought some more. Jocelyn was not obviously shy, yet she sometimes had a problem with speaking her mind. She finished her glass of wine and went back into the kitchen to prepare her mackerel.

Parker had not eaten.

Parker had not eaten anything.

Nada. Nothing. At all.

Parker was nowhere to be seen but Jocelyn didn't realise this as she was not looking for him. She would not have seen him even were he able to be seen. Jocelyn was lost.

Picking over her mackerel, made more delicious with the addition of the chilli, garlic and lime drizzle she had made, Jocelyn continued to dream.

'Maybe I should send him a message,' she thought. 'Wrapped up in a bunch of balloons, pink of course. Or maybe I should send him an anonymous invitation to lunch at the lovey pub by the river and then jump out of a big bunch of pink flowers and surprise him . . .'

Jocelyn could be rather winsome at times. (Many years ago Jocelyn's mother had remarked on this character trait. 'She can be quite winsome that one,' she had said before charmingly presenting the assembled family with fairy cakes dotted with shiny edible sequins resembling fairy dust - to her. Jocelyn's mother was fairly winsome herself.)

'Or maybe,' said the sensible Jocelyn to herself, 'maybe you could just ask him to meet up in the conventional way?'

'Hmm . . . But do I want to spoil the magic?' the dreamy winsome Jocelyn pondered.

Jocelyn had finished her supper and she cleared away her plate and wiped the table. She thought she should go to bed and start again tomorrow. Tomorrow is always a very good day for doing something you are not sure about, or not doing the something which you are not sure about, until you are. Or not.

Having prepared her night time drink ('rose petals and lavender tonight' she thought as she was still in an extremely pink mood) she picked up Parker's plate. 'Strange, he hasn't eaten anything.'

'You okay Parker? Parker?'

But Parker was still nowhere to be seen. The apartment was extremely small so he could not be far away. Jocelyn took her steaming cup of rose petals into her bedroom and looked around for her beloved Parker.

He was not in his usual dozing spot on her bedroom chair. He was not under the bed. He was not on her dressing table stool. He wasn't anywhere. He wasn't.

'Parker? Parker?'

Jocelyn went back into the sitting room and found Parker squashed into a corner between a bookcase and the wall. Barely enough room for him, but he was there.

Jocelyn picked him up gently and took him to the kitchen and popped him into his basket.

'There darling,' she said. She tipped out a few biscuits into his pink bowl (incongruous for a boy cat, but still) said 'Night Parker, sleep tight,' and turned off the kitchen light.

Jocelyn hopped into her bed, drank her rose petal infusion and sank into a sleep filled with dreams of a world where everything was pink, apart from a group of grumpy flamingos who were all green. (And not only green but the wrong green. A hard glaring green.)

In the morning, when Jocelyn went to the kitchen to make her tea and open the back door so that Parker could go out onto the little balcony to attend to his morning ablutions, she noticed that Parker was decidedly not himself. He walked in an old gentleman way and although he was indeed an old gentleman, he always had the bounce of a cat far younger in years than he actually was. Stiffly, Parker walked onto the balcony.

Jocelyn put Parker's breakfast into his bowl, ate her own yoghurt and banana 'thing' (as she called it) and went into her bedroom to prepare for the day ahead.

'We will go to the café,' she called out to Parker. 'A latte will do you good.'

Ablutions dealt with all round, Jocelyn and Parker left the apartment. Neither was particularly bouncy.

'Good morning Señorita,' called Ramez as they entered the café.

'Good morning Ramiro,' replied Jocelyn as the pair went to their usual table.

'Ramez,' said Ramez as he signalled to Ramiro to prepare the au lait and latte.

Ramiro carried the two cups of steaming coffee over to the table and set them down.

'Good morning Señorita,' he said to Jocelyn. 'You are early today, 'owsa things?'

'Fine Ramez,' she replied. 'Yet things are not quite what they seem today - in fact as I am not sure how the things are, we decided to come for an early coffee and see how the things turn out.'

'Ramiro,' said Ramiro. 'Parker is'a not'a lookin' 'imself today.'

'No, but I am sure the latte will help. Thank you.'

Jocelyn sipped her steaming au lait. Parker looked at his cup and turned away from it.

'Parker is'a not'a lookin' 'imself today,' said Ramiro to Ramez. 'Do you think'a 'e would like'a an'a amaretti biscuit?'

'Ramiro you are'a so thoughtful. But do cats like'a amaretti biscuits?'

'I donna know, yet Parker is'a no ordinary cat. 'Ow many cats do you know who like'a latte?'

'Good'a point.'

'Besides which he like'a that 'ummus you slipped 'im'a the other day.'

'True.'

'So lets'a see,' said Ramiro and took a plate of amaretti biscuits over to their table.

'Amaretti,' Ramiro said as he put the plate of little biscuits on the table. 'Special treat'a for you Señorita, an'a you Parker. Enjoy.'

'How charming,' said Jocelyn to Parker as she dipped one into her au lait. 'Such lovely people.'

Parker was not interested. He could not face anything.

He stared out of the window.

Jocelyn re-joined the train of thought that she had been on yesterday. About Bernard.

Funny how they had never met. Funny how they got on so well. Funny how they could talk about most things. Maybe that was because they had never met? Maybe it was easier to talk about all sorts of things when you don't have the other person sitting in front of you? 'Or is that bonkers,' she wondered.

Jocelyn drained her au lait and prepared to leave.

'Not touching your latte Parker?'

She signalled to one of the twins that she would like to pay.

Ramez brought over the bill and Jocelyn put the money in his hand. She knew how much it would cost. It always cost the same.

They always had the same.

'Thank you Ramiro,' she said.

Ramez shook his head but said nothing. This was not the day for merciless pedantry.

'Parker is'a not'a feelin' 'imself today, Señorita?' he asked.

'No, he doesn't seem to be quite himself.'

'He was'a not'a 'imself yesterday.'

'Oh, don't you think so?'

'No Señorita. Parker is'a a cat of taste. Parker loves 'is latte. Yesterday he not drink'a 'is latte. Today he not drink'a 'is latte. Parker looks, 'ow you say, under the weather.'

Jocelyn helped Parker down from his chair. She took a long hard look at him. He looked decidedly peaky. He looked thinner that a few days ago. He looked like a squeezed out bagpipe. He looked, well, flat.

Jocelyn carried Parker back to the apartment. She decided not to go anywhere else or do anything else today. She would monitor Parker. Today was about Parker. Her beloved Parker.

A long time ago Jocelyn had thought that when Parker finally died she would get a little dog. A little fluffy scruffy black dog and she would call him Noah Hemingway and they would live happily together. She knew she could not replace Parker with another cat. There was no other cat like Parker. Parker was a one off.

They spent the afternoon quietly. Parker took up his position between the bookcase and the wall. Jocelyn pottered around.

Later that day Jocelyn made Parker another favourite meal. Boiled chicken and rice. He loved boiled chicken and rice.

Parker ate nothing.

Parker barely moved from this position between the bookcase and the wall.

That night Parker slept between the bookcase and the wall.

Outside the less sophisticated cats were wailing. Cats always know when one of their fellows is poorly. Cats know quite a lot really.

In the morning Parker looked terrible. Jocelyn put him carefully into the little wicker cat basket and took him to the vet.

'If this is his time,' she sniffed, 'his time to go, then I will not pump him full of medicines.'

The vet looked at Jocelyn kindly. Gently, very gently, she felt Parker's tummy and looked at his teeth and his eyes and, extremely even more gently, took some blood to test in order to find out what the matter was.

'Parker is a very special old cat,' said the vet as she went out of the room to test the blood.

Jocelyn and Parker sat miserably on the floor.

'I do love you Parker,' Jocelyn said and Parker, in his way, let Jocelyn know that he loved her too.

The vet came back into the room.

'Well, rarely have I seen such excellent bloods in a cat as old as Parker. I think he just has a tummy bug.'

The vet gave Parker an injection of something to make him feel less poorly.

'I should expect him to be back to his old self in a couple of days,' she said.

'Nothing serious?' asked Jocelyn.

'No my dear, nothing serious. At least I don't think so. It can sometimes be hard to tell but see how he goes.'

Jocelyn and Parker left the surgery. They walked back past the market and Jocelyn bought some tuna. Parker simply adored tuna. Parker would, if he could, do almost anything for tuna. He would dance a fandango if he thought it would mean a tuna supper.

Sure enough, when Jocelyn put the tuna in Parker's little pink bowl, he approached it. He took a sniff. Tuna. He took a little nibble. He took another little nibble. He took another little nibble. He could not eat it all as he was still feeling rather poorly, but maybe things were on the up.

That night Parker gave up his position between the bookcase and the wall and slept in his basket.

Over the next couple of days Parker's health continued to improve. He and Jocelyn stayed in the apartment and gradually he started to look more like his old self. More of an actual pillow than an empty pillow case. On the third day he managed a little swagger.

'Right,' said Jocelyn. 'I think you are ready for an outing.'

They sauntered along the road to the café. Ramiro and Ramez were delighted to see them. They had missed them both.

'Señorita, Parker. Lovely to see you. Howa'ya doin'? Hmm Parker?'

Ramiro brought the steaming cups over.

'Au lait Señorita, an'a latte for you Parker.'

'Thank you Ramez,' said Jocelyn, smiling at the twins.

Parker took a long sip of his latte.

It was delicious.

Life felt good.

Jocelyn did not allow herself to daydream on that day. She did not think about Bernard. She decided to curb her musings, or at least to make sure that she mused at the right time. And dealing with Bernard, or not dealing with Bernard, would just have to wait.

Were this a piece of musical theatre, this would be the point in the show when the cast would step forwards, approach the fourth wall and, holding hands and in harmony, sing a moving song of love and trust and things like that to the audience.

But this was not a piece of musical theatre, but it is a story of love and trust. It was a day as any other, but a day in which the order of things had been restored.

Parker was well and Jocelyn had retained her mind.

When Parker and Jocelyn got up to leave everyone smiled. Ramiro and Ramez and Jocelyn smiled and Parker, in his way, smiled too.

Ramiro and Ramez (being of a latin persuasion) hugged Jocelyn in a manner which was unusual. They stroked Parker gently. They had grown extremely fond of the dreamy winsome girl with the long hair and her majestic cat. They bade them both a fond farewell for the day. (After

Jocelyn and Parker had left, the twins sat down with a coffee. 'Phew, that was'a close,' they said to each other with their eyes.)

Jocelyn and Parker left the café, heads and tails held high, and started on their way home. They passed the market where Jocelyn bought some squid - enough for both of them.

'I could never replace Parker,' she thought out loud to herself as she mounted the iron staircase to the apartment.

'Noah Hemingway or no Noah Hemingway, Bernard or no Bernard, you can't replace a friend like Parker.'

Advice from a Friend
Alf

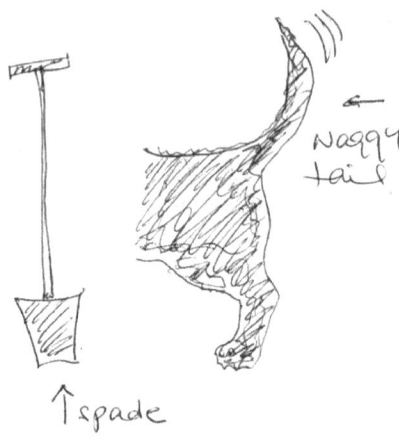

Alf was digging the road in Criffenue, a little hamlet close to where the Elf lived. She was walking that way one day and spotted him. Alf was not a young black lab, yet although his hair was showing the grey and his tummy was rounder than it should have been he was beautiful, and the Elf loved him. Not loved but LOVED.

'Alright Alf?' she called. Alf turned and saw her coming towards him.

'Alright Elf?'

'What are you up to here?' she asked.

'Ah wewl now,' he snovelled, leaning on his spade and wiping his brow with a muddy paw. 'The Gassers 'ave been workin' in the road and the 'umans and other creatures 'oo live 'ere are pretty fed up. The Gassers move one slab to 'ere,

and then back to there, and then its 'Alf clear this up wiwl ya?' And then the Gassers go off for the day and very little 'as actually 'appened.'

Alf went on to explain that the humans and other creatures who live in the road leave their houses in the morning and go off to the World of Work, and when they come home in the evening they stand around scratching their heads wondering what had been going on, as quite clearly nothing much had.

'And how about you Alf,' asked the Elf. 'How are you?'

'Bit 'ungry,' he replied.

'Well let's go for lunch at the caff, my treat,' said the Elf.

'Don't mind if I do,' replied Alf, and he put down his tools and they went off, Alf trotting at the Elf's side, tail a-wagging.

'Alf you are a Wise One,' said the Elf. 'Sometimes I wonder what the point is of all of this.'

'The point? What do you mean the point? You ge' up, you do your thing whatever that is, you go 'ome, you eat and you sleep. And then the next day you ge' up and do it all again.'

'Yes but why? For what reason?'

'Are you 'avin' a Crisis of Purpose Elf?' asked Alf (who had puffed out his chest since the Elf had called him Wise).

'I'm not sure, maybe,' replied the Elf. 'I think there must be something wrong with simply getting up, doing our *thing, going home, eating and sleeping and then getting up and doing it all over again.'*

'Wewl maybe there is,' said Alf, 'an' of course I do more than that. I live with 'Umans after all. They feed me and I answer the door. If there are rogues and wrongdoers in the garden I bark very loudly. It works both ways. F'rinstance, a few nights ago there were three 'ooded jays in the garden intent on no good. I barked and they ran off, frightened by their own shadows. And don't forget, 'ad they managed to get inside the 'ouse they would 'ave 'ad to get past me.'

'Yes but you are a big softie,' smiled the Elf.

'You know that but others don't. And my bark is VERY FIERCE.'

They carried on walking towards the caff, enjoying the late autumn sun.

'Well I am glad to hear you do more than just the every-day-ness of it all,' said the Elf. 'What else?'

'Wewl I sit, I obey, I roll over and ge' my tummy tickled and as I say I bark at the right time.'

'Yes but that's just kowtowing,' interrupted the Elf.

'But that'll get me through,' said Alf.

'Through what though?' asked the Elf.

'Through food and work and yes, if you like, the every-day-ness,' replied Alf. 'Look, I am a Dog. I 'ave these 'umans and work colleagues. I could, if I wished, live 'appily day to day simply pleasin' my 'umans and work colleagues and not thinkin' of anythin' more than that.'

'Well, why don't you then?'

'Cos if I did, I would probably go mad. There are bigger fights to fight. Bigger fish to fry. (Oo, I fancy a fried fish.) But there's no point in figh'in' a fu'ile fight - so we work, we eat, we go 'ome . . . and we wait for the Right Moment.'

'Right Moment? And what about the Gassers you work for? If what you said earlier is correct then they are the ones who get it wrong and you are not doing anything about that.'

'That would be the wrong battle,' replied Alf. 'When the time comes we will all Rise Up. Labrador workers, 'Umans, Elves and Other Creatures. But Elf, remember this,' he added as they approached the caff, 'you 'ave to be In Charge of the Moment. F'rinstance, tonight I will make my 'uman trip up. That will be fun for me. She won't get 'urt but it will serve as a reminder that I am not the serf I appear to be. Sometimes I need to Make a Point.'

Alf was drooling now as he viewed the menu. 'Go'a be fried fish aint it?' he winked at the Elf.

Addendum

Once Alf, Alf's human and the Elf had been on a most enjoyable walk in the woods. (Alf's human and the Elf were very firm friends indeed.)

There was a small stream in the woods in which Alf had been splashing about, much to everyone's amusement including his own. Lodged in the small stream was half a tree trunk which Alf was determined to dig up. (Dogs hailing from Labrador, Labrador dogs, customarily try to drag very large things around. This is because in the past they were used for dragging the fishing nets stuffed with fish in from the sea, which although a hard task they did expertly and for so doing were well rewarded by their owners. This accounts for their strange need to carry things around which are really rather too big for them and also their constant desire to seek to please humans.)

'It's way too big for him, why does he do that?' said Alf's human, shaking her head.

'Because he can?' replied the Elf.

Alf winked at the Elf.

Because he could.

More tales from Derek the Farmer
Follow the Leader

The chicks arrived in a box.

They were very small.

They were one day old.

Derek popped them into another box. One that contained a heat lamp and water feed.

Each day the heat lamp lit itself for an extra minute.

Day by day the chicks grew bigger, and as they grew bigger Derek gradually (and without the chicks noticing) increased the size of their box.

After a few days Derek changed the box entirely.

In the heat of the day the lid of the new box would open a little so that the chicks (who were becoming slightly larger chicks) could smell the fresh air.

And in the evening, as the day grew colder, the lid would close tight and the chicks would snuggle down.

The new box also had 'pop holes' which opened by the power of sunlight, and soon the chicks, being highly inquisitive, started popping out through the pop holes to leave the safety of their box and investigate the world outside.

The chicks were not afraid of the world outside. In fact they loved it. They delighted in scritching around in the dust and discovering new things to play with and eat. The worms were a delicacy, and being too small to deal singlehandedly with a wiggly wriggly worm they invented a cunning game of tug of war. They pulled the worm in their little beaks and stretched it tight in the way you do an elastic band until it, the worm, snapped. Not an image for the squeamish amongst us but a chick has to eat, often by dint of its own foraging. T'was ever thus.

When the sun started to sink and the temperature dropped a little, the chicks would return home. But how did this work? Did Derek round them up? No.

* * *

Derek was terribly excited. Madge, his best Tamworth, had had piglets. A lot of piglets.

Madge was not a young sow and over the years had become one of Derek's favourites. Madge and Derek had huge respect for each other and had grown extremely fond, each of the other.

After a recent conversation they had had one evening regarding the adult chickens who had taken over Jim's sty, Derek had re-housed the interlopers and given Jim's sty a lick of paint in an attempt to cheer the old boy up. Madge was as fond of Jim as she was of Derek, and not long after the re-furb had started visiting Jim again, often in the wee small hours when the rest of the farm was asleep. She would stroll into the sty, cheroot in trotter and a small bottle of absinthe in her trench coat pocket. And not long after these nightly visits . . . piglets!

Derek was therefore rather tied up with the piglets and had little time to round up an unruly herd of baby chicks. Derek had his work cut out chasing the young piglets around their pen and trying to avoid sliding into pig mud ('Yay, Derek 1 Piglets 0' he would yell triumphantly on the days he left the pen unsullied). So, all in all, he could not be responsible for shepherding the chicks home.

Fortunately the chicks were born with an innate sense of togetherness. And when the sun started to sink and the temperature dropped slightly, one of the chicks would decide that she had had enough, turn on her foot and start hopping homewards. One by one the other chicks would notice this off-hopping . . .

'Hey Doris. Where's Doris going, cheep?'

'Dunno, cheep.'

'Hey Doris, where's Doris going, cheep.'

'Dunno, cheep.'

'Doris? Where's Doris going, cheep.'

The questioning continued from chick to chick until one at the front managed to get hold of Doris.

'Hey Doris, cheep.'

'Yes Doris, cheep?'

'Where are you going, cheep?'

'Going in, cheep.'

'Doris is going in Doris', said Doris to Doris.

'Doris is going in Doris,' said Doris to Doris.

'Right, cheep,' said Doris.

'One in, all in, cheep.'

Situation sorted.

Catching up with Gerald - the kindly Small Spider of an altruistic persuasion who we have met before.

Relocation, Relocation

Where is Gerald?

Gerald was pretty fed up.

He had spent hours weaving that web. Hours. It was one of his more intricate ones and he had been extremely proud of it. There was a special place right at the top left hand corner of the beautifully spun dodecagon for the sleeping quarters. Most of his family spun the more conventional octagonal webs but Gerald was an inventor. And he was adventurous, and he liked to amuse his beloved Beattie and inspire his children. What a spider.

So Gerald had finished his latest web and the family had been residing there for several days.

Until yesterday. The Elf who inhabited the space below Gerald's rafters had done something. She had been watching Gerald. She respected Gerald and she left him in peace, but yesterday she had needed to do something. She had to water the garden.

The hose was just beyond Gerald's web and although she had no wish to disturb him, she knew she would have to break one of the long silken threads to be able to get to it. Gingerly she poked the silk with a trowel handle. Pinggggg. The thread was dislodged and Gerald swung precariously. Making sure that there were no other threads in her way (as, much as she admired Gerald, she had no desire to have him in her hair) she was able to reach the hose and pull it out from beyond the web and so water her garden.

The next day Gerald was not in his web. The web was gone. Completely disappeared. Looking up the Elf spotted him on a rafter. He did not move. Gerald rested on the rafter all day.

The following morning, whilst making her tea and peering through the window into the garden room, she spotted him. He had started to re-build his web. It was in its infant stage and the Elf watched as Gerald spun and twisted the little knots which he wove at the corners so that he would know where to turn around and start again and so complete his complicated pattern.

But. Someone was coming to help the Elf that day. Jeremy. Jeremy arrived and having downed his tea set about preparing the way so that he could get on. He needed to get to the plug in the garden room behind the web and . . . and he simply dashed Gerald away with a flourish of his screwdriver.

The Elf was devastated. Gerald was dispatched into a geranium. How rude.

Gerald was subsumed by pink. For several days he lay there. Shattered. He was shattered. Not that his body had been, but his dreams of building the most fancy web possible were.

Beattie was shattered. The Elf was shattered. (Jeremy had not been shattered. 'Eh?' he had said when the Elf had screamed 'nooooooooo mind Gerald . . .' Jeremy had simply carried on with his work not seeming to realise what had happened. What he had done. The Elf had sat down. Shattered.)

And for days the Elf saw no evidence of new web building activity going on. Nor did she see Gerald. Anywhere.

* * *

Privately, alone, Gerald considered his future. Not only his future but that of his family. Should he up sticks and move out? Take the family somewhere else? He had grown fond of the little Elf who shared the garden room. He had grown fond of the Big Bees who came in and out with their dusty yellow pantaloons. His family were well and happy and his youngest, Byron, was already becoming an expert in web building and was used to these particular rafters.

As we have established, Gerald was not only an artist in the whole web weaving business, but he was also very bright. He had not seen Jeremy again. Jeremy had not returned. Gerald therefore deduced that Jeremy's visit had been a one off. He shuddered as he thought of Jeremy and the cavalier way he had wielded his screwdriver.

Suddenly Gerald got it. A plan. He knew that the Elf would need to water her garden again and again. He also knew that the watering apparatus did not exist on the other side of the garden room. Relocation was the answer. By George yes.

'Beattie. Pack up love. We are moving.'

'Not leaving our beautiful home? Oh woe,' Beattie snivelled into her handkerchief. 'We have been so happy here . . . The children are used to the peculiarities of this place . . . oh woe oh woe oh woe . . .'

'Calm down love. We are moving yes, but only across to the other side - the other side of this garden room which we love so much. My cousin George who used to live over there has moved to his own particular choice of pastures new, leaving his entire space vacant. It will be an adventure and there are no risks of watering activities wrecking my webs. We will be cosy and safe and happy.'

Gerald folded his front pedipalps in a Taa Daah moment.

Beattie rushed to embrace her husband and called the children to whom she explained the plan.

And so it was that Gerald and his family, weaving as they went, crossed the rafters and moved into their new space. Beattie tutted at the state of the place - George was clearly not obsessively compulsive in the cleaning stakes, but Beattie's own obsession enabled her to create a home for them all which they would grow to love. And to love almost more than their previous home.

A few mornings later the Elf was sipping her coffee in the garden room and turned her face to avoid being blinded by the sharp sunlight. And then she spotted him. She would know that spider anywhere.

And impossible as it is to discern a spider's smile, the Elf knew that there was one. A very broad one indeed.

The lady felt lucky to have met so many extraordinary people along the way . . . and she admired their creativity, as some admired hers. The lady had found this wonderful sculpture particularly captivating and both she and Russ had shed a tear when they got to the end of the story.

Sitting Room – the Mantle Piece
Sculpting Wings

Ned leaned against the fence watching the young ones tearing around the field.

He wasn't particularly jealous. He'd had a good life.

'Merryweather is looking handy,' he thought to himself.

He mooched over to where Russ had set up his easel.

'Ned old boy, how are you doing?'

Ned nuzzled into the bag. Same procedure. He picked up a shiny red apple and munched it.

'Looking good, Ned,' said Russ.

Ned slowly lowered his body and took up his position next to the easel. Same procedure. And so another afternoon passed blissfully - artist painting the scene with the old horse lying like a labrador next to him.

***

Russ and Ned had met a couple of years ago - after the accident.

Russ had moved to Portbrid a while back. Having become bored and suffocated by life in the city he had sold up, opting for an altogether quieter existence.

The move had been liberating. Swapping the citysmoke for the fields and rivers and hills had nourished his soul and given him the space he needed to allow his mind to wander. And his work had developed in a way altogether different from its previous direction boxed, as he and it had been, in a conventional corporate environment. He now lived in his own world, populated by the dragonflies and hares he liked to draw. But Russ was not yet a total hermit and a little desire for the hustle and bustle of city life stayed with him, and he liked to wander into the town twice a week on market days. On those days he would pick up the provisions he needed and chat to the market traders and enjoy a pint in the local pub. On one such occasion he overheard a conversation John Tanner was having with someone he didn't recognise.

'Breaks my heart,' said the someone he didn't recognise. 'But what can I do? He's no good to me anymore and I can't just hang on to him. My beasts must earn their keep.'

When the someone left the pub Russ followed him out.

'I couldn't help overhearing,' he said. 'I may be able to help.' Thus, Ned had come to live with Russ.

Ned had been a working horse.

He had worked all his life. But then the accident had happened. He would have been retired soon enough - but the accident had put an abrupt end to his career.

The farmer had checked the bolts - or at least he thought he had. No one could have stopped the massive machine which Ned was pulling from going down the side of the hill - taking Ned with it.

A broken shoulder. He had been lucky to escape with his life. But a broken shoulder rendered him useless to the farmer - and so he had to go.

Russ had a small paddock which backed on to the fields beyond, and this was the perfect retirement home for an old nag.

Ned had been delighted. He had been saved - he knew only too well the probable alternative. And so he, too, now lived a peaceful life and he and Russ became firm friends.

But in the evenings he liked to run. 'Run'. In reality he 'ran' at a gentle trot, sometimes managing a canter - but in his mind he was galloping at full speed . . .

Oh how he used to run.

But now this giant horse of a horse trotted about, dreaming of days long past.

Sometimes, in the dimpsy inbetween light of an afternoon becoming an evening, Russ would watch the old horse trotting around the field and smile. In the daytime Ned was as stiff as an elderly arthriticy human - but in the nearly darkness he seemed as ambulant as a young stallion. Which was odd.

But things were set to change.

Nothing remains the same. We know that. We all know that. But often we allow ourselves to live in a little bubble of Hope - or Denial - because it is easier than facing up to the inevitable.

Russ first noticed something was wrong when Ned appeared to be more troubled than usual with the flies. Damn flies. They got into his eyes and he seemed unable to shake them off.

The next day Russ appeared in the field carrying an old straw hat into which he had pierced two slits for Ned's ears to poke through. He pushed the hat firmly onto Ned's head. Brilliant.

A few days later Russ noticed that Ned was having trouble munching through the customary apple, so the next afternoon he arrived with an apple ready cored and cut into bite size chunks. And so it went on, Russ noticing the slight changes and always thinking of a way he could help the old boy.

But one evening as he watched Ned from the house, he had a shock. Ned was not trotting around the field. He was not trotting, in fact he was barely walking. It seemed as though all the energy had finally drained from the old horse. It broke Russ' heart to see him like this. There must be something he could do? And then he smiled.

He had been working on a pair of wings for a clay model of a unicorn. The next morning he arrived in the field carrying a strange pair of wings created from willow wisps and catgut fixed to a yoke he had found in the barn.

The day passed peacefully in the same way as always - horse lying at artist's feet. And when it was time to leave Russ fixed the yolk across the old horse's shoulders.

'Night Ned, fly well.'

In the morning the old horse was no more.

Wherein the Elf, the Most Marvellous Musical Major and their new friend the extremely small fieldmouse, having had a peculiar time, encounter an extraordinary encounter.

The Door to the Brave New World is Closed

Some strange forms were emerging.

Forms not distinguishable as will o the wisps nor the cloud formations which turn into cats and faces and dragons. No. Grey shadowy forms as if whoever or whatever they were had fallen into a pot of potty putty or chewing gum and had not taken the time to clean the muck off. So they appeared covered in stuff akin to the slime coating of the Alien as he blasted through Sigourney Weaver's stomach wall.

Grey shadowy forms.

The Door to the Brave New World was closed. Not only closed but an enormous creeper had wound itself around the door, latch and hinges, swamping all in spikey greenery. In fact the door was barely recognisable as a door. It could have been a monolith standing vast and alone in the nothingness. On close inspection anyone with decent eyesight might just discern the panelling and door furniture - the long iron hinges and the latches and locks. And the padlock. An enormous padlock that hung from the oversized door handle. A padlock yet a rusty padlock. In fact everything was rusty. Rusty and old and creeperclad.

Silence.

There was only silence in this strange nowhereland. The wind did not whistle through the creeper branches, the wind did not whistle at all. There was no wind. There was only stillness and silence.

If as well as decent eyesight you possessed a large silver ear trumpet or a hearing aid of the very latest technology, you may however have heard a something. A very small something. You may have heard the tiniest snuffliest noise. And then if you magnified that tiny snuffly noise by the power of twenty seven and a half, you would have furrowed your brow and wondered 'what on earth?' And this question would only have been answered had you x ray vision which is asking quite a lot of a human or other creature. However, if you did have x ray vision you would have seen through the creeperclad monolithic door to the other side of it, and on the other side you would have seen a peculiar sight. A jumble of a someone with a powdered wig and powdery clothes (which on later inspection turned out to be a rather fine doublet and hose in fetching purple and green) slumped at a table, snoring, head cocked to one side like a robin, but not. Smiling beatifically to himself and breathing snorily and snufflingly. And you would have deduced by the powdered and powdery wig and dusty doublet that he had not moved for some time.

* * *

Somewhere in the distance the grey shadowy forms were moving or gliding - and as neither you nor they could see their feet, if they had any, who was to know? They glided and moved and glided some more, moving silently through the silence. As they moved on and on the ectoplasmic gooeyness gradually started to dissipate. On and on they glided or moved shedding little bits of albumenesque stuff as they glid.

(At this point if you had a powerful telescope and happened to be pointing it in the general direction of wherever it was that these grey shadowy forms were gliding or moving, you would have thought that these grey shadowy forms were cloud sculptures of some description. If you had all the things which have been mentioned within these and previous words you would be a very peculiar sight yourself. Perhaps you are - we may never know unless you show yourself.)

As the grey shadowy forms glided or moved on and on, and as the sticky goo continued to drop off, they became less grey shadowy form and more human or other creature form and finally, finally as they glided or moved seemingly upwards and the last droplets of goo had left them, we see them exposed as the whoever they are. And what a funny sight of whoever they are, they are. An Elf, a Most

204

Marvellous Musical Major and an extremely small fieldmouse.

Now that the trio were no longer bound and gagged by stickiness they were able to talk to each other. They sat down on the nothingness and shared a sandwich.

'Do you think we are going the right way?' asked the Elf.

'No idea,' replied the Most Marvellous Musical Major.

'Right way or wrong way we are going somewhere,' said the extremely small fieldmouse, 'and somewhere far away from the No Where Land we have been living in.'

'But this is a nowhereland too,' said the Elf.

'True,' said the extremely small fieldmouse, 'yet an empty nowhereland, unlike the No Where Land we have left behind which was positively teeming with far too much of almost everything.'

'Meaning?' asked the Most Marvellous Musical Major.

'Meaning,' replied the extremely small fieldmouse, 'that this is a nowhereland empty of the thieves and liars and blackguards and RATS!'

'Ah yes, how true,' replied the Elf.

'And how wonderful,' replied the Most Marvellous Musical Major, and he did a little dance and played a trumpet.

A trumpet major naturally.

* * *

As they were now completely ungooed and had reverted to normal, as normal as an Elf, a Most Marvellous Musical Major and an extremely small fieldmouse were able to be that *is, they surmised that they must be close to the Brave New World.*

They spotted a door hanging in the nothingness - a massive creeperclad door with enormous rusty hinges and a huge padlock dangling from the door knob and made their way up to it. They knocked politely - even though they realised they could probably have gone around it as there were no walls or floors or ceilings to restrict movement.

Nothing happened

They knocked again.

The door creaked open in a non spooky way.

'Ah, hello no longer grey shadowy forms also no longer covered in ectoplasmic Alien type slime,' said a sleepy looking powdery bewigged someone dressed in doublet and hose.

'Oh, hello. I hope we have not disturbed you?'

'Hmm, I may have been asleep for a while. We don't get many visitors these days.'

'We?'

'Um, yes. Me and the Door.'

'And you don't get many visitors these days because?'

'Because it seems many humans and other creatures have stopped looking for a solution to their problems, stopped even believing that there might be a solution or that they can change things, and have become covered with the Grey. The Numb . . .'

'Oh no . . . Like the person in the waiting room who shrivelled to nothingness. Like Geoffrey in the Town Hall.'

'Actually I am Geoffrey. How do you do.'

(Aside. This must seem to you to have all happened extremely swiftly. One moment the trio were covered in slime

and oozing their way through the nothingness and now they had been hurtled into a conversation with a sleepy doorkeeper who turned out to be Geoffrey. But they were quite accustomed to having to catch up with curious situations and to them this situation did not seem at all curious. In fact, quite the contrary. All in all this was a pretty normal day.)

'Geoffrey . . .' said the Elf, aghast. 'What on earth happened to you?'

'I went through the door.'

'No Geoffrey! You mean the creaking door in the Town Hall? You mean you gave up Hope?'

'Yes Miss Elf. I gave up Hope so I went through the creaking door. But you know, the Zombie Keeper of the Door is actually a really nice chap, once you get beyond the filthy bandages and his breath smelling of the grave.'

The trio settled down on the nothingness sensing that this could be a long story.

'Go on Geoffrey.'

'Well. Hmm Hmm. Once the creaking door closed and I was on the other side of it, the Zombie Keeper of the Door took me through a tunnel of bright lights and offered me tea and cake.'

'Tea and cake? You mean you had completely given up Hope, you numbly walk through the creaking door and were given tea and cake by the Zombie Keeper of the Door?'

'Yes. Earl grey and Battenberg actually. Jolly nice.'

'Jolly nice,' agreed the extremely small fieldmouse.

'And then the Zombie Keeper of the Door unravelled the bandages from his face. Turns out his name is Nigel and that's his job.'

207

'Job?'

'Nigel?'

Yes job. Yes Nigel. Jolly nice chap. He explained to me that he had been unable to find a job in the outside world and that he himself had given up Hope and passed through the creaking door to find the position of Keeper of that particular Door vacant. He told me over tea that a similar situation had become available here, as Keeper of the Door to the Brave New World.'

'So you couldn't get a job through the Town Hall, completely gave up Hope, went through the creaking door and . . . got a job? That's incredible.'

'So does everyone get a job who passes through the creaking door? If so, and were it to get out, it could just about ruin the Town Hall's modus operandi.'

'No not everyone. Apparently some humans and other creatures who have a tiny bit of Hope left have the Auras about them.'

'The Auras?' quizzed the Most Marvellous Musical Major.

'Yes.'

'And you did Geoffrey? You had the Auras about you?'

'Yes, I still had the merest snippet of Hope. A tiny morsel of Hope lodged behind my left ear. Might have been left over from that cuppa we had together Miss Elf. So yes, the Zombie Keeper of the Door told me about this job which I was very pleased to accept, even though fewer humans and other creatures come this way these days due to the Numb.'

'The Numb?'

'Yes.'

'Hang on . . . what happens to the humans and other creatures who do not have the Auras about them? For whom all Hope is gone?' asked the Elf.

'That is too terrible to think about and almost too terrible to recount,' replied Geoffrey happily recounting. 'They pass through the creaking door and, as I say, the Numb takes them.'

'Takes them where?'

'Don't ask. Anyway,' he continued, 'why are you all here?'

The Elf, the Most Marvellous Musical Major and the extremely small fieldmouse told Geoffrey about the conditions back in Old London Town. How humans and other creatures had forgotten how to do their jobs properly, how nothing worked, and how Money seemed to be King and how humans and other creatures lied and cheated. How the three of them had become increasingly fed up and disillusioned with waiting for people who they thought were the Right People, but who invariably turned out to be the Wrong People, and how when things went wrong no one took responsibility and anyway no one cared.

They told Geoffrey about how they had all met - the Elf and the Most Marvellous Musical Major having been firm friends since the Most Marvellous Musical Major had helped the Elf in the selling of her house and the buying of another one, and how the extremely small fieldmouse and the Most Marvellous Musical Major had met on a particularly nasty Friday afternoon on the steps of the House of Pain where the Most Marvellous Musical Major worked. On that particular Friday the Most Marvellous Musical Major had

had a protracted session with the Rats with whom he had to deal on a weekly basis. The Most Marvellous Musical Major had become increasingly fed up with the foul and rotten behaviour of the Rats. Not a day would go by when he didn't throw his eyes heavenward and plead with the whomsoever might be listening to save him. The Rats were running the housing market and the extremely small fieldmouse had had a strong desire to take over, but that had turned out to be really difficult, mainly because as she was so extremely small many humans and other creatures could not believe that she could be tough enough to take on the Rats and win. She certainly could have and would have.

They told Geoffrey that one day they had simultaneously screamed enough through their windows and decided to get together and discover the Brave New World. They had read about its existence a long time ago and had agreed that it had to be better than continuing to live miserably where they were. The worst thing about living where they were was that many humans and other creatures had forgotten to remember The Important Stuff and, more significantly, they had forgotten to remember that they had forgotten to remember The Important Stuff.

So here they were. Floating somewhere in a nowhereland of nothingness but eager to get on and enter the Brave New World and forge a new and different future for themselves.

'My dear, nay, very dear friends. I have important news for you. You may need to sit down,' said Geoffrey.

This sounded worrying.

The trio sat down.

'I stay here, behind the Door, waiting. I wait for the rare humans and other creatures who, such as yourselves, have travelled in Hope of finding the Brave New World.'

This sounded ominous.

The extremely small fieldmouse gulped.

The Most Marvellous Musical Major wiped his brow.

The Elf frowned.

'But, my new and very dear friends, prepare yourselves. The Brave New World does not exist.'

Silence.

Silence.

Silence.

No one moved.

'Did you hear me?' asked Geoffrey, The Keeper of the Door to the seemingly non existent Brave New World.

No one moved.

'The Brave New World does not exist,' he repeated.

'No No NO NO NOOOOOO,' cried the trio in harmony. 'You can't tell us that. We all have Hope. Our Auras must be glowing. We are ready to start again in The Brave New World.'

'But if it doesn't exist,' said the Most Marvellous Musical Major mournfully.

'Hang on, if it doesn't exist then why do you have the permanent position of Keeper of the Door to the Brave New World?' asked the extremely small fieldmouse.

'Quite so, and how did we find you?' added the Elf.

'Well we more or less pop ourselves wherever we think that anyone who is looking for the Brave New World may find us.'

'We?' (they ask again.)

'Yes, me and the Door.'

'Eh?'

'We get wind that someone is coming through the nothingness, and using my trusty slide rule we estimate the likelihood of that someone or those someones passing in a certain direction and then we pop ourselves somewhere in the way.'

'That is very odd.'

'No more odd than you believing there actually is a Brave New World,' said Geoffrey, huffily.

'So you say it does not exist. What on earth and in any other corner of the Universe does that mean?'

'It does not exist in the way you want or expect it to exist.'

'Eh?'

'The Brave New World does in some ways exist and in other ways it does not. It exists within and without you, in real and absolute terms, but not as another land to which you can travel and start again.'

'You mean . . .?'

'Yes.'

'Not . . .'

'Yes. Change must come from within. You have to search for the hero inside yourself . . .'

'Oh that is such a disappointingly old cliché' said the Elf.

'Maybe, but a cliché is only a cliché as it is a collection of words which have been passed down through the ages . . .'

'Maybe so, but isn't it time for something new?'

'. . . ahem. And a collection of words which have been passed down through the ages have only been passed down through the ages because they are worth listening to and taking notice of.'

'So. This nowhereland of nothingness which we thought was the entrance to the Brave New World . . .'

'Exists only in your minds. Go back. Make a Brave New World where you actually live. Change your world from within. But hurry, the Numb awaits . . . and never forget, as one door closes . . .'

The voice of Heather Small is heard singing in the distance.

* * *

The trio found themselves suddenly back on the steps of the House of Pain. They looked at each other, and without exchanging words had precisely the same thoughts.

They didn't know if they had dreamed the adventure, or whether they had indeed been gliding through the nothingness in the nowhereland. Had they been floating like Joseph of Arimathea through and upon the mists of Sedgemoor as he went to plunge his staff into Wearyall Hill to create the original thorn tree of legend?

Or was that too fanciful?

Whatever and whatever whichway, they resolved to do as Geoffrey had suggested - to make changes from within not without, and do their best to withstand the assaults of the liars and cheats and blackguards and RATS. They decided that they would, the very next day, open an Agency that the extremely small fieldmouse would run. The Most Marvellous Musical Major resolved to give up his job at the

House of Pain and work with the extremely small fieldmouse in an attempt to bring some honesty and proper values back into the business of buying and selling houses and the Elf promised to tell everyone hither and thither about the new honest Agency. And do their typing. They also resolved that wherever they found cheats and vagabonds and wrongdoers they would tell those humans and other creatures exactly what they thought of them and expose them wherever and whenever they could.

It would be hard, but there were three of them and change is always easier and a million times better when you are working with dear friends.

Addendum

Our three intrepid and hopeful explorers had begun to prepare a Manifesto for use and proclamation after they had entered the Brave New World. And even though that were not to be, it would seem churlish not to share with you, so may I offer you:

Manifesto for a Brave New World (a work in progress.)

1. **No shouting.**
2. **No cackling.**

Anyone found shouting or cackling will be taken to a field where they will have to shout or cackle for four hours.

3. **Loud music.**

Whereas loud music is of course a joy for those who are listening to it, it should not interfere with other's lives. Anyone found playing loud music which does interfere with other's lives will be taken to a small room and have Black Sabbath music played directly into their ears for four hours.

4.   *No dropping of litter*.

Anyone found dropping litter will spend a day following four children who will drop litter and be forced to pick it up for four hours.

5.   **Consideration**.

Anyone found behaving in a selfish and inconsiderate manner will be taken to the House of the Common People and have eggs thrown at them for a total of four hours.

Finale

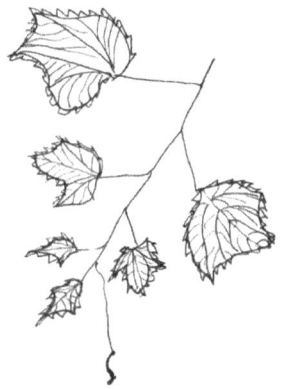

Crispin was confused

The lady had cut the vine.

Cutting off his access to food and stuff.

Was he alive? He didn't know. The lady didn't know.

Would he twirl up and find himself?

At this point no one knew.

COME ON CRISPIN.

The Caterpillar hung there.

Nothing was moving.

Not one of his probable or possible sixteen legs were moving.

The lady went inside.

Crispin had to be left alone.

This was mega stuff.

Damn.

The Next Day

The lady realised that Crispin wasn't a caterpillar at all - rather a little bit of detritus left dangling in the vine after the chop.

And the lady also realised that she would not have noticed this before now.

So why now?

She had not retired, she doesn't have endless hours to ponder the survival tactics of a caterpillar.

No.

She is still plotting her own course.

And yet, and yet . . .

Crispin's potential had her thinking . . .

If we had more time, that elusive gift nowadays . . .

Or if we chose to spend our time differently - wouldn't that be a good thing?

Wouldn't we wish we did have time to watch a caterpillar wind his way back up a twig?

Or watch a teardrop of rain as it glides down a window pane?

Are we all chasing the wrong goals?

Dunno.

Do you?

* * *

And as the lady sat in the garden room pondering non-Crispin's non fate and the various possibilities of her own, she thought about how much had been achieved since she had moved into The Little

White House. How much achieved, and how much given away. The non-achievement of the shop - the futility of many of the battles (her elf brain winced) the enduring friendships she had and the fact that The Little White House was still standing regardless of other humans' meddlings, and that she was happy. And she decided that instead of trying to avoid uncertainty she would become open to it - to all its vagaries and wonders. And also that at times we have to accept ('ouch', elf) when certain battles can't be won - no matter how hard we try. 'You can't make water run uphill Amanda,' she was once told - and it was true.

'The next part of the journey may not be the one that I had envisaged,' she said to her other brain 'nevertheless we are on a journey and like Colin Dragon and The Most Marvellous Musical Major we are going to have to be prepared to bend like the willow (if you see what I mean).'

Tea?

Addendum

The last conversation between the brains that day, as the lady wondered if she were losing her mind.

'Am I losing my mind?' she asked her other brain.

'On the contrary, you have simply found something in it which you had previously not noticed.'

'And what is that?'

'A Disregard.'

'Eh?'

'A Disregard for things which do not matter. A Disregard for things you have left undone which you previously thought ought to have been done. A Disregard for humans and issues that want to bring you down or do you ill. Need I go on?'

'I have?'

'Yes. You may not realise it now but you are on the very brink of a new reality.'

'Sounds scary.'

'On the contrary, it will be liberating.'

The lady sat down. She needed a think, but before she settled into her think her other brain piped up again.

'You do not need that think,' it said. 'You simply need to relax and see what happens next.'

Appendix

With grateful thanks to these artists who have allowed me to use their work.

Goodbye to a Rainbow by the Art Class at Eltandia Hall Care Home, Middle Way, Norbury.
The Hour Glass - from The Koestler Arts Trust Exhibition – unknown Artist.
DAYWBDB by Zonnewende
The Value of Fluffles - Lithograph.
Unknown Artist.
A Moment of Peace - Unknown Artist
Pollyanna by Charles Newington
Stay Clear of Armley - Graffiti - Unknown Artist
Once upon a Time in The Land of Hidden Tears by Zonnewende
Pigs out Til Eight by Rosanna Morris (from the 2019 LWA Calendar)
Girl in a Café - Spanish - Unknown Artist
Follow the Leader - Ceramic Plate
Sculpting Wings by Russ Snedker
All **elf drawings** by yours truly.

Other books by Amanda Brooks:

Of Humans & Other Creatures – Book I – My
Desperate Year.
The Earl and Countess
Trawling The Century (Jane Brooks, Amanda
Brooks editor).
Curious Tales of The Rag Bag – in collaboration
with Zonnewende

Some Reviews of Book I

What a delight to discover a fabular novel in the old-
fashioned English tradition: quirky, full of a sense of
folklore and individual in every respect. Added to
which, and unlike many, it has lovely line illustrations
which are witty and imaginative - little vignettes which
accentuate the idiosyncrasy. Ted Few – Antiquarian.

It is astonishing in its originality and concept, with a
comic sense of the ridiculous in dealing with the
tedious everyday stuff which affects us all. There is
always hope! And to coin a phrase, "I didn't like it - I
loved it!" RJB. Poet

A brilliant book but hard to categorise! Is it
autobiography? (Yes) Is it social comedy and satire?
(Yes) Is it drama, fantasy, comedy or tragedy? Yes. All
of these and more. The writer's imagination is amazing
as she takes off in spirals of surreal fantasy that are
absolutely original and full of vitality, energy, and
wisdom. I love the way she moves from fantasy to
reality, weaving them together in a tangled and highly
coloured web. Above all I love the humour and her
marvellous way with words. Anne Merrick. Author.

Milton Keynes UK
Ingram Content Group UK Ltd.
UKHW051834101223
434126UK00004B/26

9 781999 703158